Job Shadowing

Job Shadowing
Malcolm Sutton

BookThug
Department of Narrative Studies
Toronto, 2016

FIRST EDITION

Copyright © Malcolm Sutton, 2016

The production of this book was made possible through the generous assistance of the Canada Council for the Arts and the Ontario Arts Council. BookThug also acknowledges the support of the Government of Canada through the Canada Book Fund and the Government of Ontario through the Ontario Book Publishing Tax Credit and the Ontario Book Fund.

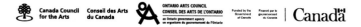

LIBRARY AND ARCHIVES CANADA CATALOGUING IN PUBLICATION

Sutton, Malcolm, author
    Job shadowing / Malcolm Sutton.

Issued in print and electronic formats.
paperback: ISBN 978-1-77166-202-4
html: ISBN 978-1-77166-203-1
pdf: ISBN 978-1-77166-204-8
mobi: ISBN 978-1-77166-205-5

    I. Title.

PS8637.U886J63 2016   C813'.6   C2016-900589-5 | C2016-900590-9

PRINTED IN CANADA

Shelfie

A **bundled** eBook edition is available
with the purchase of this print book.

CLEARLY PRINT YOUR NAME ABOVE IN UPPER CASE
Instructions to claim your eBook edition:
1. Download the Shelfie app for Android or iOS
2. Write your name in **UPPER CASE** above
3. Use the Shelfie app to submit a photo
4. Download your eBook to any device

For Bossie

There is no parting from your own shadow. To experience this faith is to know that in being ourselves we are more than ourselves.

—Bernard Lovell

Classplaza

The teens will eventually break away from Etti, though in the minutes I stand watching them no one wants to take the first step. They are lingering, giving hugs to each other, recording goodbyes on their phones, their parents waiting at a thoughtful distance with their car doors open. In the hazy evening light that softens everyone to orange and brown I can see that Etti has a glow about her as she always does on these occasions.

I used to participate in Etti's projects when I was between contracts, being helpful in the background, sort of there and not there, but now I stay clear. This time I left for a few days because Etti said she and the teenagers would be doing something constructive in the space - like building an as-yet undetermined structure. Together they would decide what to make.

Over the years she has sought out places that are more and

more like voids, as though she needs to challenge herself more, push her practice, intensify the experience for the students. Her most recent proposal led us to this unit that she has named Classplaza. We inhabit the space, and she works from it – a long narrow room beside a number of similar industrial park units, still clad in the dark wood panelling and drop ceilings of its original days. The front is a massive pane of glass beside a heavy glass door, all framed in aluminum. We have it for a month while she brings in suburban high school groups to do open-ended projects. She is attracted to these cold and inhuman environments, she thrives on them, even finds aesthetic pleasure in them. To her they open a window onto something new. At least she forces herself to believe they do, and I think she actually does believe there is more possibility in them than spaces already won over by life. Like others who see potential in the bleak abandonments of past decades, she is able to revive them, at least for a time. She wants people to experience each other in a form unrecognizable to themselves. Some over-educated part of me can't help but admire what she does.

At the same time, I've noticed there is something about Classplaza that prevents me from seeing anything beyond its glass door. Though she has a horizon in Classplaza, an undefined paradigm, I can see nothing but the desert we are occupying. Maybe because she thrives on them I begin to see these deserts as an extension of Etti. I am less and less able to see her without her necessary deserts.

I slip away from the goodbye scene of Classplaza, the sky steadily darkening, and when I return in the total dark the students have left and Classplaza is lit up inside. From the parking lot I can see that our temporary home is filled with a sprawling construction made of pegboard, cardboard and string, surrounded by metal-framed office chairs from the '70s or '80s. Stepping inside, I see large sheets of paper taped together and covered in notes and doodles and diagrams. The composition fills the main space of the unit, and I imagine Etti must be somewhere behind it, near the kitchen area, back at her computer.

When Etti hears me she says, We didn't have time to disassemble it before they left. They were a great group. I'm always surprised by what they come up with. It always amazes me.

I can hear, even in her enthusiasm, that she is beginning to crash. Physically and emotionally she is exhausted. She throws herself entirely into her work and then is spent.

I don't ask Etti about the week with her teens. I know what kinds of things would have been discussed, where Etti would have encouraged them to go and what she would have steered them away from. She once said to me that no one is ever taught how to work together, and in this realization a world of possibility opened for her.

At the back of the office I find our futon and pull it into the front area, dragging it upright past the student construction. I lie down, and among the sketches that adorn the cardboard see strings pinned from one thought to another, triangulating into webs. I get up and pull away a folded sheet of cardboard from the main construction, and Etti hears me and tells me to wait. I might want to take some pictures still, in the morning, she says.

I recognize Etti's handwriting in one of the clusters of notes: *How might we work together: as two, as three, as four, as five, as six, as seven, as eight, as nine, as ten . . .* Alongside 'as two' is a drawing of two figures holding each other hand to ankle in a tumbling pose, rolling forward. Below that is a drawing of people leapfrogging each other toward the mouth of a chasm. Written vertically up one wall of the chasm is, *What is this place?* It all looks very searching, tentative, a step toward something else. Without thinking I begin to take apart the construction again, then catch myself.

Etti comes over to a tripod set up a few feet away from me and removes the DSLR, taking it back to her computer where she will upload the images from the week, documentation of the project with all the scenes of teens working together and talking and building, and images of Classplaza from the outside, its white vinyl title, *When We Work in 3 and 4 Dimensions*, adhered to the glass front.

I'm ready to settle into a book when she picks up from a conversation begun a few days ago. She says, Sometimes you have to do things that you don't want to do. She is speaking about how I spend my days. Sometimes any movement is good movement, she says. And I think, it is because I don't understand how my life fits into the working world. But I say to her, I've often done things I don't like to do. And I leave it at that. I think of those things that I've done, which appear as fragments floating into the past, each fragment populated by incidental people who paid me or worked alongside me. There is no thread connecting the fragments together. I would like to say something more to Etti, something optimistic or even enterprising, but I can no longer picture a future self going about life in a fully formed world.

In another era not long ago, we might have planted ourselves in a commune and home-schooled long-haired children. What an image, I think. But pictures like these have come to me increasingly over the months and years. My parents were not involved in communes, intentional communities, back-to-lander farms, marches on capitals, underground plans. Most of their generation were not involved. But it seems as though that was their story. I see childhood memory-images of my father's colleagues at the university. I smell the old university offices and chemistry labs. Somehow this is where my mind inevitably goes: the labs of universities, the farmland of communes, even though they seem to have no place whatsoever in this industrial park and in this life that Etti and I share.

Soon we will have to leave this place that she has named Classplaza, but this time, unlike most times, it is not clear where we will go. Despite her clamouring, nothing has come through for Etti, no funding and no spaces. It's clear that she needs a break from her work, but a break is impossible. We have nothing to fall back on. And there is another feeling too: that we have faulty trajectories. At this moment when life and work have solidified into one and the same action for Etti, I am farther than ever from any sustained employment. I am so far adrift from all my adult milestones.

Before we go to sleep that night, as we lay on the futon amid the cardboard and strings, she finally looks me in the face and says: There was a time when I felt really equal to you, but now I don't. Now I can't place you. I can't see where you're going, what your story is, how it is part of mine. She rolls over and turns off her light, and I leave mine on and pick up my book, which keeps me up well into the night.

Josephine

Early the next morning, I go out wearing my clothes from yesterday, ones I've slept in, and take the sloped shoulder of the road away from Classplaza. By chance I end up in a parking lot where a large group of people has assembled. The group continues to grow.

Most of the people are quiet. They seem to be strangers to each other, but I feel right away that I can't so easily add myself to them, as they are for the most part in their twenties and formally dressed. But I do join them. Perhaps it makes me feel less conspicuous to be among them than on their periphery. I want to know what's going on so close to where Etti and I are staying.

A van pulls into the parking lot, and after the motor is turned off a minute or two passes before two older people, about my age, get out and approach the group. They introduce themselves as Petra and Troy. Welcome, they say. We will be taking you to Learning Ecologies. Follow us. It will be a twenty-or-so-minute walk.

Having heard this I decide to leave. But then a woman from the crowd, very much my age, exchanges a look with me. It should have no lasting power, yet it does something as simple as acknowledge my presence. She goes along with the group and I follow at the tail end.

We slowly spread out into a fractured line as though it is natural to do so, as though trying to get away from each other in the gentlest or least hurtful way. Without giving thought to it, a group naturally dawdles and always desires to spread out, having begun close together to listen to its leaders. We would come together again at intervals, or at least at the destination, I imagine, and togetherness is better after a break. We are always changing our minds, adjusting, recalibrating. The closest person must be seven or eight feet away. Farther than conversational distance, but not so far that I feel outside the group.

The woman my age then appears beside me. She tells me her name is Josephine.

She reminds me of people I've known in the past in what now seems another life. A past period of my life, but also a different decade of human history altogether. I need to say something to fill up this space that she's created, however small it is.

I went for a walk this morning, and I ended up here, I say.

You must have walked a long way to get here, she says. She stares at me rather than gesturing to the low flat buildings and empty parking lots that surround us.

I'm staying nearby. Temporarily, in a plaza.

Oh, she says. Are you one of the organizers?

With this? I say. No.

You are part of the program then.

No, not that either.

Do you know why everyone is here?

Not at all.

You just like to tag along? To meet people?

I don't know what to say. Honestly, I'm not sure, I say.

I tell her that people don't put me at ease, but it is also true that I seek them out. I like to be near people but not too near. I open right up to her. I say that when I come into a room of strangers, at a conference for example, or something like this very group, I become quiet and fall into studying the others in the room. When we go around in a circle and say a few words about ourselves, when we say what we do, when our self-interest and current fixations – which are often the same as everyone else's – surface, when all our passions announce themselves, it becomes clear that there is far more to us than I want to hear. The others are accomplished. They have degrees, successes, pursuits with good intentions. They are not enemies at all and ought to be friends and collaborators. But they are, after all, competitors in some imagined pursuit.

I don't feel that way towards this group yet, I say. I don't even know why they are here. Why would I be competitive with them?

Everyone here is quite a lot younger than you, she says.

And you too, I say, and she smiles. I ask her what this is all about, all these people gathered on this walk.

A job opportunity, she says. A kind of job shadowing for an educational organization called Learning Ecologies. Educational programs outside of schools.

And you're going to job shadow?

Yes.

At your age? I ask. It just comes out.

Yes, at my age. And she pauses, clearly hurt, and we continue to walk in close proximity. I've often thought about jobs I've never performed and what they'd be like, she says. Like a dental hygienist, cleaning people's teeth all day, every day. Or an ultrasound technician, pressing the thing into your ribs or groin and clicking at intervals, looking for dark areas on the monitor.

How do people do that all day long? But I don't have a job, so I don't really know how anyone performs any job all day long. Which brings me here.

Job shadowing it is, then, I say as though everything has added up. But all I can see is the giant ring of blindness surrounding what she has just described.

Last night I was reading the story of a writer driving solo across America, from New York to LA, to meet with a production company interested in making a movie of his novel. It was by someone who must have come of age in the late '50s or early 1960s. At first I was in awe that he makes the story of himself seem as though it is the only thing going on in the world or, rather, not the only thing, but that other things in the world are there simply to add texture to his own life. There is a right-wing couple from Texas that he runs into, for example, who seem surprised that he's driving through Texas unarmed. They ask him to handle their gun, to feel its weight, before he drives on to California. The interaction is a brief episode that he throws in before leaving it in the past.

It's true, he tells us, that his mother warned him there is much to fear in the world, but this danger perhaps adds just another texture to his experience rather than being a disabling force. The idea that there might be things to fear just creates an exterior world against which he exists, a backdrop, and in fact acts as a part of what enables him to focus on himself. This story was not about things to fear in the world, but about him. And then

I thought, why should I think about this now? Why does this example stick out to me? Isn't this what most writers aim for: to push the rest of the world away in order to focus on one thing? On one line of motion? On a single arc of life? That is how themes emerge, that is how we create a story of love or death or generational dissent. In the case of this man, he was allowed to focus on a particular conflict: the trouble working with others who are business people rather than artists, on a Hollywood adaptation of his novel *The Men's Club*.

He and I are so different, I thought last night. It doesn't matter that he is a great and famous writer, and it doesn't matter that he is dead. That's not the difference. What matters is elsewhere. I started reading another story in the collection but kept thinking about what the difference was, whether it was a quality in me or something else entirely. And then I thought of something, I tell Josephine.

She is patient. We walk along shoulder to shoulder on what is either a street or a very long parking lot.

This thing that I couldn't place at first – the thing that differentiated me from him – was not a failure to make myself the centre of my own life story and not a failure to shut out the world, but the very impossibility of shutting out our present world. My parents, I say, their generation was able to shut out the world. For them, shutting out the world was a way of owning it for themselves. They were able to invest in things that were distant and invisible to them in order to exploit their own story, their own freewheeling life's highway to the fullest. And they made incredible stories for themselves that seemed to encapsulate the idea of freedom. And we as their children grew up with this vision of life.

Josephine listens to me. We walk along a few feet from the others. I share my ideas with her as though it puts them to the test.

For us, I continue, I think the world encroaches. The world encroaches so much that there is no individual story strong enough to shut out the world, there is only the encroaching world that makes a story so difficult to tell, or that prevents us from having a story in the first place. The individual trajectory is devoured by it. The author of *The Men's Club* could hold it at bay. His generation could hold it at bay. But I don't think that we can. Or maybe we are faking it when we try to keep it at bay.

Josephine lets time pass before saying anything. She has an uncanny ability to walk in a straight line while maintaining eye contact. And her openness, verging on a kind of purity, I feel I'm exploiting. I have my doubts about what I've said, but at the same time I feel like it goes far to answer a question that has been creeping deeper and deeper into my grey matter. And I don't know what I am expecting from her, when she says: I wonder if what you have to say is overly general. I don't mean anything by this, but I suppose the writer that you are talking about was a man. Maybe he was white too, and maybe together these qualities created a human that was able to move with such ease through the world and shut out what was unwanted. When she says this, Josephine doesn't seem angry or even critical. I think she is just curious. I just mean that maybe some could hold it at bay, she says. Maybe others it overwhelmed, the way you're saying it overwhelms you now. I don't think my mother held it at bay the way that you say this writer did. Probably lots of people didn't.

Before I can reply, our leaders Petra and Troy call us to a halt. Troy says to our gathering group, Everyone . . . Everyone . . . if I can get your attention . . . We forgot to mention at the start that at the conference centre there will be a number of other groups from different organizations, also here to shadow. But don't worry: there are enough spots for everyone. We should be arriving at the centre in a few minutes. In fact, you can see it from here, and he points at a reflective glass building not far off.

My last job, Josephine says as a gap opens again between us and the others, well it's not really possible to say last job. There have been so many small jobs that haven't added to a bigger job but that have sustained me while I do other things. I work when it comes my way. I have not been very practical. The shadowing feels practical somehow. Structured. I've become set on it. I'm actually dead serious about it.

I believe her. I feel the charge that comes with being surrounded by new people. Her dead seriousness surprises me but also charges me. She makes me feel something that I cannot place. A kind of equality that I don't often feel with strangers.

But she must have seen something less positive in my reaction. Perhaps I gave away a look of disbelief, a look that told her there was no way I myself would job shadow. We continue in silence.

Our group slows outside the swelling overhang of the building. The glass structure looks brand new, slightly in advance of anything I've seen before. It seems to have landed here from outer space. Petra and Troy climb a few of its steps to gather our attention. I just want to say thank you for your time, Petra says. We'll be leaving you here. Good luck with the rest of your day. All best, Troy says, and waves his hand. All best, Petra says too. Please, she says, and gestures to the doors.

We all go inside and orient ourselves to the space. Grey and brown dots moiré up the glass walls of its foyer, drawing the eyes up to its vertiginous, breathtaking, transparent ceiling.

You should definitely do this, I hear Josephine say. Change is good, she says. And when I look back down to her she is heading to a hallway that must lead to the washrooms. I'm ready to return to Etti and Classplaza but feel wrong about not saying goodbye to Josephine, especially after her final words, which linger as an invitation to follow her. I had not considered shadowing. It had not crossed my mind in relation to my own life.

Within a few minutes the foyer amasses young women and men, obstructing my view of the hallway to the washrooms.

The scene is mesmerizing, not just for the congeries of youth, all flesh and new clothes, the job-interview-style jackets and pants and ties, but for the morning light that blazes through the glass wall making everyone appear tinted, a little translucent, like smoked-glass vases positioned on a credenza. The bustle makes it seem like opportunity awaits everyone.

I work my way through the expanding numbers down the hall-way where Josephine has gone. Since she's not in the line of women waiting outside the washroom, I think that she may still be inside. I linger near the entrance.

The woman at the front of the line makes a few exaggerated sighs. These women in their twenties, half my age, I think. Their whole lives in front of them, their parents would say. So young, but so old to be in the business of job shadowing. I memorize the sighing woman's appearance, comparing her to the other women behind her, and note the distinctive label stitched to her rear pocket: 'Entre Nous.' She advances around the curved wall then disappears from view. In the time it takes her to pee and check her appearance in the washroom mirror, surely Josephine will have finished, having been farther ahead in line. I imagine that this young woman will somehow flush out Josephine. But after ten minutes the sighing woman emerges, rushes past me, and there's still been no sign of Josephine. After a few more minutes I leave the hallway for the great glass entrance, and find a place in line at one of the welcoming tables, thinking, really, I should be going.

At the front of the line the greeters ask my name and I tell them that I haven't signed up, that I was just tagging along. The team of two smile and say, Not a problem at all, and ask me to write my name and address on a list. You were with the Learning Ecologies group? And I take out of my wallet the square of paper with my Classplaza address and copy it on the sheet, going along with the soft officialdom of it all. They give me a folder and a black bag silkscreened with the Learning Ecologies insignia. Write your name on this tag, they say, handing me a Sharpie, and when I'm done I slip it into the plastic case and clip it to my shirt. As I turn to leave, the woman on the right says, Wait, sir, we need to assign you a table and seat number. She hands me a small card with 325-6 printed on it.

Amid the circulation of bodies born in the '90s – young to my eyes, but not so young that they look like children, more like smoother versions of myself – I look once more for Josephine. It is really time for me to leave, I think to myself even as a number of the interior doors open, the doors that must lead to the conference hall. I have no place to be, but it is time to leave. Yet the crowd carries me through into the hall, a gigantic dark space. Tables are laid out in a honeycomb pattern so that it is impossible to tell if the walls are mirrors or if the room just continues on and on, in failing acuity. All discrete boundaries between one person and another seem erased, tablecloths and shirt sleeves becoming extensive with each other, blazers and T-shirts, pants and table legs, chairs and people, the carpet and the wall indistinctly meshing like an endless wedding reception. After some wandering and standing and gazing across the room, after some getting up on chairs to see over the heads of others, searching for my table number 325, but more than that for Josephine, I find my assigned seat. Others join me at my table and we nod to one another. Soon the lights dim and a spotlight hits a lone podium onstage. The entire room becomes quiet, and there is electricity to the quiet.

Etti

Used to working in view of the public, as they completely ignore the people occasionally walking past them. Three men focused and calm, setting event speakers on pole stands, then a fourth skirts past them looking for something. They do it at a slow pace, without speaking to each other, two of them with their concern directed at the floor, while the other unravels a cable. A shallow stage at one end, cables extending everywhere. One of the men, Etti observes, has tattoos from his ankle along his calf to the back of his knee. She can't make out what they depict, and moves closer, and one of the images appears shinier than the others, glossier, gleaming red even in the poor light. There are tattoos everywhere she goes, but this one is fresh. It must be new. One more image brought into the world, she thinks. She takes a few more steps toward him, following the line of the arcaded colonnade. Even though she is preoccupied with something else, she wants to see what a new tattoo looks like, one decided upon very recently, not from an earlier, younger self, but one from this week in 2017. The guy is now helping out another of the crew with a folding stand, trying to set up a mixing board, the two having difficulty, the mixing board not fitting the stand though the crew remains calm as if there is no problem. They are pushing and pulling, mixing board and stand, leveraging the stand, then one puts the mixing board on the floor and they turn the stand to its side and work the folding X back and forth, scissoring it. They continue without frustration, used to being in view of a public that for the most part ignore them as they stroll past on their way to the art. Or so she likely imagines, as there are not really people strolling past, not at the moment. It's like choosing something for your skin, she thinks, mind still on the tattoo, or deciding against all other things for your skin. But how does it connect to all the other images, all the TV and movie and still images? she wonders. And to art. How does it relate to what I do? She moves away from them, removes herself from the scene, stands behind one of the columns that line the interior square. There is not much of a reason for people to go around this way, it's kind of a dead space in the museum, and she begins to feel that she sticks out, but like the men on the floor she is also used to doing things in public and doesn't mind the thought of sticking out. She knows that no one will care unless they are paid to care. Someone would likely eventually care within a few hours because there *were* people paid to care in the museum, but paid to care only after a while, to see if there is any problem and then ask pleasantly enough to move on. The light is bad in the colonnade part, and in the centre as well, the crew work in dimness, and she lets go trying to see what image the installation guy had finalized into his skin in the past few days.

The wall between columns has a plaque on it, and the next wall between the next columns and so forth all the way around the interior square. These plaques are what she has come for. 'First Founders' heads the first one, and names, individuals and couples, drop below as a list, so many names that at a glance none sticks out, and she walks around the square, counter-clockwise, each plaque engraved with a different variety of founder heading their lists, Visionary Founders, Transforming Founders, Landmark Founders, and then Grand Founders, Distinguished Founders, Patron Founders, and Founders with no descriptor. They might just as easily have been found on the museum's website, she supposes, but she has come here in person, she has not been to this museum in a long while. She walks around the periphery a second time. First, Visionary, Transforming, Landmark, Grand, Distinguished, Patron. A ranking related to the size of donation, of course. How much per rank, exactly what range of donation? she wonders. It is important. It is the thing that distinguishes one plaque from the next, but the information given is just the category, Visionary and the rest, and not the size of donation. The range probably grows exponentially, so that if the first group donated in the hundreds of dollars, the next likely donated in the thousands, the next in the upper thousands, and the next in the ten thousands, maybe the next in the upper ten thousands and the next is the lower hundred thousands. Then upper hundred thousands, then presumably a million mark is met, after which the zeroes are so numerous they cease to matter. And she realizes it must be more than just money distinguishing the groups. First Founders, where she stands now, those people are surely dead, surely long dead, because the museum is old. The museum is newly renovated though, so many of those under other headings would still be alive, having given to recent fundraising campaigns without which no renovation would have been possible. Now she recognizes the name of a local business owner who is alive, so far as she knows. She sees Michael Snow on one list, and wonders if there are other artists too, perhaps like him donating work for a silent auction to raise money for the renovation. She doesn't really know how these things work. At First Founders she begins again and descends through the ranks, counter-clockwise, taking photos of each plaque. The flash goes off and in its wake the room goes black for a second. As her eyes dilate, readjusting, it looks up at her: the tattoo that must have been inked a few days ago. A woman emerging from something cylindrical. She goes closer, sees a pinup style woman popping out of a giant cake, stares at it for some time as the man tries to undo a knot in a cord. She stares and sees that there is text on it too, written across a banner that the woman holds aloft, but she can't make it out. She moves on. At the Landmark Founders again she reads down the list and moves on, now attracted to Transforming Founders who would likely be very recent ones contributing to the renovation. Least likely to be dead, most likely to be full of a quality she realizes only now she is looking for: aliveness. Merely being alive, she likely thinks. But something else too. A quality that would compel the person to donate to a renovation when a star architect is involved. What was that? A desire for revitalization? A faith in the near-future? These titles are all very godlike, she thinks, like they are there to signify a club of titans. She's been taken in by this lexicon of metaphysical leadership, as an aesthetic experience, and has been somewhat overwhelmed, blinded by the words. Now she tries to rein in her reaction.

She once read that intuition is a method, not a hunch that comes from an unknown place within like the gut. It is a process of disinterestedness that allows you to see better while at the same time elevating your sympathy to whatever the world offers. Insight through becoming like the situation itself, through actually *becoming* the situation itself, yet asking nothing of it. Like so many things that she reads and doesn't fully understand, she applies it to the way she works, to find out what it means through trial and error. So she tries to let go of the founders' titles and her desire to pinpoint a particular name on the lists. She tries to be present in the warmest but most detatched of ways, putting away her camera, taking a step back, becoming part of the museum wall. She hears sounds filter in from the reception area. A man and a boy step past without noticing her. The men continue setting up the audio gear. She wanders the square, closely passing the workers as though she were invisible, trying to take in everything at once. Though there is no way for her to let go of being a player fully invested in the situation, still she tries. Maybe something does change for her.

Now she returns to the lists and one name begins to glow for her. She has no idea why. But she lets it happen, she commits it to memory. When she glances again at the men working, the tattoo comes into view. The outlined woman holds a banner with the words 'Spaceship Earth' written across it. And it is out of view again.

At home she uploads the photo files to her computer. The images appear harsh from the flash, hot sunbursts making some of the names illegible. She skims through the lists but knows the exact one she will arrive at, then searches the internet and, remarkably, finds an email address for that one name, the name she intuited to be *the one*. She sends the proposal to him that she wrote several days earlier, on the day when Gil took off without a word and didn't come back.

The flight to Helsinki allows time for doubts to inch in. She thinks she may be in over her head, that what she has proposed is beyond her capabilities. She becomes more and more surprised that the man has said yes to her so quickly and without questions. But high over the Atlantic, she has committed to a single direction. So often her future is like this. Increasingly this has become her way of life.

The morning after her arrival, sunlight illuminates the white sheets of her hostel bed, waking her disoriented body and sending her onto the street searching for any shop that might be open. When she enters a convenience store, she forgets what she has come for and stands before a newspaper rack in reverie, as though the newspapers are new to her, as though each one is somehow better than it would be elsewhere, merely by its foreign setting. The *Financial Times*, the *Guardian Weekly*, and *The New York Times*, and then all the others in languages she doesn't know. The last time she bought a paper was before they went online, for a review where her name appeared in passing. Still, she knows the *Guardian Weekly* and *The New York Times* but not the *Financial Times*. She's never held a *Financial Times* before, but the pinkness of its paper attracts her this morning, it goes with the coffee cup that she imagines in her other hand, the reason she came into the store, and the quiet park bench she imagines occupying. The man at the counter stares directly at her as though he hasn't seen a woman in days. She takes the *Financial Times* to the counter and asks the man, having already glanced around the rest of the convenience store, whether they sell coffee.

Yes, he says. It is not a very good coffee. At this time of day you would do better at the Central railway station.

Oh, she says.

Do you know where it is? he asks. Perhaps you could get me one too? It's about 1,200 metres from here. I can point you in the right direction.

She hands him the newspaper and a large bill and says, Which way? and he provides her with change and leans over the counter so that their views align, so that their cheeks almost touch, and points through the window, up a sloped street, and tells her at the top she will be able to see the distinctly modernist building by the large square. Stone men hold big balls on either side of the front doors, he tells her. It is unmistakable.

She thanks him and heads in the right direction, holding the newspaper like the pink hand of a friend, and soon spots the train station where a few minutes later she purchases two coffees. As she heads back to the convenience store she takes a different route, wanting to see another street, and angles away past a church and a cemetery park that she hasn't seen before, and stops on a bench to drink her coffee, letting the other get cold and feeling bad about it, and it really bothering her for the next hour or so. She thinks of the pale young man at the convenience store.

Having retrieved her backpack from the hostel, she takes a northern pastel street past early morning workers who seem strangely happy, if groggy, then hikes along treed streets with gated embassies, arriving at the dock where she buys a ticket to the island of Suomenlinna. A small ferry transports her and a handful of other passengers, likely people who work in the bistros, ice cream stands and museums on the island. Etti has read about Suomenlinna, a UNESCO heritage site, once military but now recreational. In a few minutes the workers walk off the ramp and disappear around a low brick building.

The island is formed of grassy mounds, this morning littered with young people passed out in sleeping bags, knapsacks used as pillows, beer bottles strewn around them. With hours to kill, she treads among the camped-out groups. Pretty much everyone is still sleeping. It smells of campfire. It is serene.

Her time dissolves: hours later she waits on the patio of a small café, aware that any man might be the one she's crossed the ocean to meet. She feels that she should document something of the meeting, if only to record her feelings as she waits. Years of practice have taught her that any event, no matter how small, could become part of the project, even if it is not evident in the final work. All things inform a work, add to it, even if those influences remain invisible to the audience. They shadow its reality. That tattoo of Spaceship Earth – she wishes she had documentation of it now, and of the men setting up the stage. She sips coffee and nibbles at a pastry.

The man will know from the internet what kind of work she does, given that countless images immediately pop up with her name, her projects all well documented and written about in blogs and journals. From these he may or may not anticipate that she'll turn her experience with him into an artist thing of some kind, perhaps one that involves teens. Still, she would act as if this were not the case, as if he had done no research whatsoever. She'd act as if no one ever Googled anyone else.

Though she has chosen a spot that gives her a near complete view of the patio, a man comes up from behind and stands over her, appearing tired but cheerful, his shirt heavily creased. He sees the folded newspaper she's been holding the whole time she's been waiting there.

Eurozone stares into the abyss, he reads out loud. We Live in Financial Times.

All the news that's fit for pink, she reponds. You are Caslon, she says.

Etti, he says. Let's get moving, it's going to be a busy day. He slips some money beneath a plate on the table and she follows him down a path to where boats are docked. They pass several wooden vessels before he gestures at a very small, sleek speedboat. He gets in and reaches out his hand. Your pack, he says, and she hands it to him. You, now, he says, and she grasps his hand and steps on board.

Take a seat at the back, he says, and hands her a long, thin piece of cloth with a metallic sheen. She holds it in her hands.

I need you to put that on.

On what? she asks.

You know, around your eyes.

Really?

I require it.

He seems to find it funny, because she seems to find it funny. She is taken aback, which manifests as laughter. They take their time thinking it is funny, together, as though stepping outside themselves for a moment.

I'd think it was funny if it wasn't happening to me, she says. I'm not going to put this thing on.

She knows circumstances like this, where decisions are made and imposed without any discussion. She always aims to divert them. And here, with this man and his strange speedboat, and this blindfold, she remembers her gender, is made to remember it and feels disappointed at having to remember it, and looks at Caslon in order to assess his investment in the blindfold, whether he might get some perverse pleasure from this simple operation, whether it is just the first of many such requirements. He merely smiles though when he says, I need you to put this on. You need to put this on.

She stands up and the boat rocks and she puts out her arms to steady herself.

Believe me, whatever you are thinking, it is not going to happen. You were the one to contact me. We both have our requirements.

She wants to wear the blindfold, acquire it, keep it for later. And this desire makes her feel younger, throwing her back into what she would have felt at art college. She looks around at the greenery and brick buildings, at the small masts of sailboats in the little harbour. Even as she mentally resists his request, an image forms for her: a woman and man as viewed from a dozen feet away, standing in a boat, the woman wearing the blindfold that reflects an overpowering sun. It is a scene of crystalline realism. She is often fond of a style dictated from the outside because she would never come up with such a style herself. The world rocks gently beneath her.

Parts of this, what we're doing, need to remain hidden from you, he says. It's just what we do. It is for everyone's peace of mind. Now please, if you will.

She remains silent. She notices, beneath one of the benches, what looks like a sleeping bag pushed into a draw-string carryall.

What's the difference, he says. Once we're out on the water you'll be isolated from everyone, blindfold or no blindfold. But really, there is no reason for you to worry. This is as much for your security as for ours.

She extends the blindfold to its full length. Its fabric is incredibly shiny, reflecting the noon light as a mirror would. She wants to own it, despite herself, because so much is already embodied in it.

There is a big difference between wearing a blindfold and not wearing one, she says. I won't see anything if I wear it. I won't know where we're going. I won't see you or the water or where we come to shore. If I say yes to a blindfold then I'm saying something. Like wearing it is all right with me. Like of all the things I might say no to, wearing a blindfold is not one of them. If we were both wearing one, things would be different.

Yes. That's a good point. Things would be different.

When she is forced to think about her work, to write about it (as she sometimes does of things in her life), she says that it requires operating in a reality as unfiltered as possible, which means no symbolism, no allegory, just life rich for its singular manifestation. So she must be open to it, whatever it is. She must be open to possibilities, she absolutely must be, especially at this germinal stage in a project.

He offers to tie on the blindfold for her. Almost everything 38 years has told her about the world urges her not to do this. She should get off the boat. She should rethink her plans. And yet, maybe this was a good idea. A bad idea *as* a good idea, she thinks. From the outside she sees a tall, well-dressed man, if slightly dishevelled, standing across from a woman who is often mistaken as younger than she actually is, holding a silver blindfold.

He takes notice of her little daydream and says, I believe you'll be perfect for this job.

She takes it closer to her face. It has a slight smell of perfume that irritates her eyes. She ties it on and sits on the bench below her.

The motor putters and the boat slowly turns. After a few minutes the speed increases.

It's Midsummer's Day today, Caslon shouts over the motor. Midsummer's Eve. Everyone will smell of bonfire tonight, he shouts. Lots of drinking tonight. The country will be drunk. That is the way people are. Drunk and on fire. He laughs, thinking this very funny. We'll have a party too. One needs to dip in among them now and then, he says. Or to be like them.

Hands fall on both shoulders, telling her to stop climbing stairs, to stop walking forward, to stand in place. She removes her blindfold, and adjusts to the ocean light.

A broad bay drops away all around. They seem very high up, with a number of storeys underneath them. She looks across the pinkish planks of a massive deck, precisely laid out like a computer model. It is the deck of a very wide-spanning yacht.

Welcome aboard the *Nancy*, Calson says.

Somewhat giddy, Etti says, *Nancy*. Hello, *Nancy*, and she

sweeps her foot across the smooth salmony wood, which extends on and on before being bound by railings, after which the world abruptly disappears.

She ties the blindfold around her wrist.

I'm so glad you came, he says. Fantastic. Fantastic of you to come. You didn't bring much with you. A backpack, a newspaper. I've had one of my men put those things in your quarters. This is where you'll be staying for a while.

Thank you.

Of course. Forgive me. Hosting is not what I excel at. I'll put you in better hands.

It all enters her too fast, unsettling her senses. She cautions herself to slow down, to take a breath, to reduce her thinking. For now, she basks in the immensity of the yacht. How she would love to share this initial impression with her friend F. It is fucked up, her friend F would say. Totally fucked up. But what is it about this that is fucked up? she asks F, who occupies a part of her brain even when they are far from each other. I guess we need to figure out what fucked up actually means. Yeah. What does fucked up actually mean? And the two of them would stare at the deck and succumb to the perfection of its furniture design, the unusual curvature of the rails, the meticulous handling of every fitting. It is well beyond them, despite their education in the world of materials and objects and contemporary thought. It is well beyond them at a technical level. It is as though every aspect of the vessel had evolved simultaneously, as a single entity. They would not know how to read it beyond the show of expertise that wealth affords, the desires of the super-wealthy materialized in their most symptomatic, out-of-reach form.

I've taken the liberty of removing your cellphone from your things, Caslon says. I've put it in a secure place. And your voice recorder and your laptop. No photos anywhere on the *Nancy*. Excuse me for being expeditious. It's a holiday. Midsummer's Eve. A timeless holiday. We like to celebrate here. There are preparations to make. Today we celebrate, tomorrow we work.

And Caslon leaves her with a man who has been standing behind her for several minutes, an employee in a white and silver suit. He introduces himself as Nelson.

A clothing rack stands inside the door of her new quarters where Nelson has left her. Dresses and shirts organized by colour, a muted rainbow, and, she quickly discovers, drawing the clothes apart from each other, all about her size. She could wear any of it, she thinks. She wheels the rack out of the way.

Spread across her bed are three full-body costumes. The first is a faux-fur panda with a hood that would partially cover the face. The second, a motley shirt and pants, tattered and stained to signify a pirate or street person or something. And the third, a slinky dress scaled to look like a snake or dragon. A sexy lizard dress, she thinks. They appear to be organized by the weight of the material and the extensiveness of body coverage, the panda being the heaviest, baggiest, and most extensive, concealing almost all of the wearer's body, she imagines, and the sexy lizard being the skimpiest, wrapping around the wearer's thighs and forearms and up over the breasts and middle back. Sexiest, of course. Her immediate feeling is likely to screw with whoever laid them out on her bed, to put on all three costumes, though she would collapse from overheating in them. She considers mixing them up: Panda pants plus lizard mask. It is all very limited. She supposes Caslon, like many men, would prefer her in the sexy lizard, straight up. But then again, she hates to prejudge. She tries to leave it open even when someone's intentions are obvious, as perhaps they are now. Because, she thinks, even if the intentions are obvious, they can be rerouted via her very openness. Openness is disarming, it compels others to change their behaviour, to step up, to be better than they might otherwise be, so she believes. She is tired, flops herself down beside the costumes, pushes the panda bear away so that it slides off the bed and in doing so feels it brush the back of her fingers, revealing not faux fur but something more natural, coarser than a rabbit or cat but softer than a horse, with a subtle oiliness to it. She closes her eyes and tries to think no more of it.

F returns to her mind, and she pictures herself showing off the costumes to her. This one? she asks F, and wonders if this is the useful dialogue she believes it to be rather than a fantasy of speaking to a friend who's not present, simply a conversation with herself. She values F's thoughts more than anyone's, more than Gil's if she were being honest. F's are less critical, more practical, more open. The salient issue, she thinks, lying on the firm mattress, dialoguing with F, is whether or not this very conversation is really with an absent friend or just with herself. She knows that a real dialogue with F would be more useful, because, after all, there is no way to predict what her friend would say. She is always guessing, acting F's lines based on all the real conversations they've had. But hasn't F surprised her too, over and over again, so that in fact there are things that F would say, many things, that she herself would never think of? One can't really think of things that one can't think of, can one? she thinks. One can only think of things that one *can* think of. But is that true? One cannot span the distance even between oneself and one's closest friend because that closest friend is someone else, completely discrete. In a way, she thinks, that's the deal. Isn't that the deal, F? That's what we must embrace.

But there is an idea beyond those she's just been considering, something most people could never imagine: that another person's view is worth taking more seriously than one's own. Yet she knows this might be true. At least she read it in an essay by an artist, and was so energized by it at the time that she incorporated it into her way of being in the world. Her own view is less credible to her than F's, because F is an utterly different person than she is. And that difference makes all the difference.

Therefore these conversations with F taking place in her head are not as useful as if they were with the real F.

Does all this mean, she wonders, following the logic that she felt was guiding the argument, that it would be better to dialogue with someone else, anyone else, in person, than with a close friend she carries around in her head. Does it mean she

should be bouncing ideas off someone present? Like Nelson?
Like Caslon? Someone she has no reason to trust?

She visualizes wearing those costumes – the panda, the vagrant
and the snake – and momentarily sleeps.

A beep wakes her, and a digital screen lights up on the wall,
across which a message repeatedly scrolls. *Please be ready in 15
minutes. Nelson will lead you to the deck.* She continues to rest
on her bed until she hears a knock on the door, followed by a
voice addressing her as Ms. Etti and asking if she would like to
prepare to be seen at the party. She asks him to wait while she
gets dressed, and when she emerges in the vagrant costume,
Nelson is standing outside her door.

How do I look in this thing?

He simply says, You look well.

She notices he has a fresh tattoo blooming on his forearm. It
looks like the symbol from an expensive handbag, somewhat
like a harp, black on his dark brown skin. Perhaps it is a brand
label. And then it comes into recognizable form: a simple dollar
sign and its mirror image, interlocking at the S curves.

What's that tattoo? she asks. You must have gotten it recently
– in Helsinki?

Oh yes, I had a couple of days on land.

And she is escorted up to the party, wondering if Nelson's opinion would be a fill-in for the absent F, but soon discovers he will state no opinions on anything. It seems crazy to her how little he's allowed to say. She considers asking whoever she meets at the party whether they think anything about the yacht or her outfit is fucked up, but things always unfold so differently in reality than they do in her mind.

Victoria

Folding away from myself, falling two-dimensionally from our table, descending then splaying across the carpeted floor of the conference hall as though enacting an adolescent trust game, I let it happen. I remained open for long enough to let it happen. I acquiesced, I said yes by doing nothing, and let the lungful of air seep free from my mouth. I lost my skin colour. Josephine disappeared from sight, and I was certain she gave me a look, one muddled in emotional equivocation, leaving me with the dread of abandonment, wondering if I'd been deceived, though I could not say in what way. Small shrieks pierced the massive hall, and ruptures of laughter, giggles, sighs of ecstasy perforated the air here and there, until a brief silence fell, after which followed the low and indistinct brush and knock of chairs and shoes, people shuffling out of the conference centre, our numbers halved.

A few minutes earlier, a man had approached the microphone onstage. He asked for everyone's attention. His name, he said, was Jan Melbrooks. *I'm a life historian,* he said with his big hands sweeping the air symmetrically and precisely. *I think about lives in history,* he said. *As part of history. Jan Melbrooks. It's great to see everyone here. Let me say a few words about myself.* And he said some things, I was distracted. My table was large, at least ten people at it. Then I heard him say, *My great teacher, my mentor, he once told me . . .*

I stopped looking around and focused on him, like everyone else in the conference hall was doing.

I've got something important to speak to you about today. Life-changing. And I think it will be life-changing if you allow it to be. But where to begin? I want to be brief but have so much I'd like to say to you as you embark on this amazing opportunity. This might be a strange place to begin, but bear with me. I'm going to begin with an old idea, one that seems to have been forgotten over the decades, but which I think should be recuperated. An image: Spaceship Earth.

The idea of Spaceship Earth came about sometime in the '60s, like so many other outbound metaphors. There were books: The Economics of the Coming Spaceship Earth. Operating Manual for Spaceship Earth. *They were premised on the notion that the earth has limited resources and that we are all in this together. We are one world. One humanity, all together and in need of a pilot. Let's forget about the pilot for now and the limited resources.*

In the '60s those two words must have been connected, in everyone's minds, to that image of the earthrise: that picture taken from the perspective of someone waking up on the moon. The one taken by the Apollo 8 crew. It shows a view of earth half in shadow, the lit-up part at the top, a planet lit from above – please use your mind's eye – somehow as if it is being born, bright blue against black, a lot of black with a little blue, and the part not blue utterly black like the background. We're interested in the part that is so important and yet cannot be seen – the shadow side of earth. That, as you can see in your mind's eye, is not visible.

And he clicked on a device hidden in his hand and there appeared that famous image of earthrise from the perspective of the moon, while he was saying,

What do Spaceship Earth and the moonrise photo have to do with us, here in the conference centre, in 2017? How about this: no objects without shadows. Those things allowed us to see that not even planet earth escapes having a shadow. Nothing escapes it. Well, maybe the sun, there is the sun . . . No shadow there. At least I don't think there is. Maybe someone could prove me wrong.

Anyway, what I want to get to, what can't be seen in this photo, what is missing, yet what is incredibly important, is history . . .

The stage lighting obscured the man's age, made his neat hair reflect inky blue-brownness and his skin glow remarkably bright white, like paper impregnated with fluorescence. Yet even as I again looked for Josephine, some of his words drilled

47

into me, penetrated my senses, because he was saying things, using a certain style of language, putting things together. . .

The second word that I want to remind you of came into popular use in North America around the same time that this image was taken from the moon. Zeitgeist.

Zeitgeist is the spirit of the age. That's what it means. It's a term about how people at a given moment in history hold a common worldview that is somehow new and in contrast to that of the near past, of their progenitors. And I believe that, by coming here today, you've decided to embrace it: the spirit of participation, of joining with others, of being open to economic opportunities that arise for you. For what are we if not what we do with our lives in the time that we live in. We must embrace the limitations as possibilities. We are realistic today, more than ever. We must embrace the reality that we are part of today.

It is so easy to hate someone when they get up onstage and start telling things to you and the rest of an audience, as though the stage-man's thoughts are valuable to everyone, as though the stage-man doesn't need anyone to question him. But I tried to keep an open mind. I thought of what Etti had said about movement. I thought about Josephine being serious about this. At the same time that you dislike the person onstage, a trust germinates and slowly grows for that person. I looked at the others across the table from me, who gave nothing of their private thoughts, who appeared calm and attentive, as though hypnotized by his fluorescence.

People used to travel to the East for self-discovery, but surely that was an attempt to escape the very zeitgeist that defined them, no matter what they discovered abroad. We know now that the East was already part of the West's zeitgeist. And today there is no more to be found in the East than there is here in this conference centre. We are more realistic than our parents who went there. Spaceship Earth is globalized. We don't need the view from the moon. Rather than going away to find ourselves we believe in staying where we are and viewing the world from another angle, another person's perspective. Let us discover what it is like on the shadow side of the global experience. Saying yes to this is our zeitgeist. Let us form a new institution that is the natural result of our time, that exemplifies our spirit. An institution of job shadows.

Faces brightened at my table. The man really spoke to the people in the room, digging up truths that they didn't know they believed in. And I realized: I can visualize being a job shadow, even though I will never do it. He allowed me to see myself as a shadow. This was the moment that I surveyed the room for exit signs and by coincidence saw what must have been Josephine's face only a few tables over. She too was glancing around and I was almost certain she caught my eyes, as eyes naturally catch other eyes.

Through the job shadow, let us discover what it is to be ourselves. The more conscious you are of yourself, the freer you will be. We will all be freer the more conscious of ourselves we become. It is our duty to each other. I am so excited for you all.

A woman sitting to my right got up from the table – a young woman whose sternness, whose apprehension, was an aberration in this hall of captivation – and every alternate person at the table got up from seated position, and every alternate person got up from every table, and then it happened.

That night a trio of Victoria's co-workers take her out to a martini bar. They give her a cupcake with a wax 2 and 3 lodged in the frosting, and one of them lighting the wicks, and they sing for her. She lets the candles melt down without blowing them out. They say, Whoo hoo! 23! and surround the martini glasses with more cupcakes and gifts bound in pink foil ribbons. They call for a round of flavoured vodka shots and nudge one another to drink in unison.

Dimly, from somewhere beyond Victoria, I take it in. It is all new. I'm compelled by how they are with each other. As the conversation unfolds it becomes clear that she is closer with Eugenia than Saleema or Taylor, and yet, maybe because the get-together is for her, Victoria seems reserved with them all. They somehow get onto the topic of men without naming any specifically, discussing the odours and body hair and shaving, moles on backs and chests. Victoria doesn't say anything about a boyfriend, and when asked if there is anyone new in her life she ignores the question. The others fill in the air by divulging their intimacies as if they were nothing at all. Then the table becomes crowded with another round of drinks, and they lose track of what they are doing, moving the chairs all to one side, a series of group selfies taken for the event. Victoria inspects the photos and asks that they don't post them online, work and all.

I have forgotten what it is like to be wobbly drunk, and before I can register what is going on Victoria is running to the women's washroom to heave her insides into the toilet. As they are leaving the bar she says to Eugenia, This is not like me. Eugenia smiles and squeezes her elbow.

Overnight she wakes in sweats, defenceless to what must have been bad thoughts or anxieties. I can't tell. She turns the light on at intervals, and glances at her bedside table where books are stacked beside a lamp and her cellphone. Before work the next day she takes a pill of some kind, scrubs herself clean and hides behind a layer of makeup. She applies some drops to her eyes and holds herself up straight in front of the mirror. The effect is miraculous. It says, I'm here and ready to go. That day she interacts minimally with her co-workers, who are at desks in the same little room, only feet away.

Before nausea emptied her that night, I'd anticipated that she'd mention me, or that she'd allude to the job shadowing program that surely the others too were involved in. I thought eventually it would come out. But even plied with drinks she kept it to herself, said nothing of me. I wondered if she were ashamed of her situation. Perhaps she was obliged by Learning Ecologies to remain discreet, but I have no insight into what led to all this.

A few days later she says to Eugenia, on the other end of her phone, I'm closer to a window now than I've ever been. She's come home from work, but still in the same clothes and at her computer. I can see past the divider, she says, and through frosted glass to the window. I can't really see anything of the outside. But still. There is light, natural light.

This is all true, I think to myself. It is so strange to be moved so early in the shadowing. I silently agree that it's a better view than before.

Does the move mean anything? Eugenia asks.

It's the same job. But a new desk. A different computer monitor, slightly bigger. A little duller in contrast to the brighter room, Victoria says. My view has changed. A new horizon. I mean, it's really like having a new horizon. They didn't really tell me why, she says. They just said they were doing some shuffling. What do I know? When they tell you something so vaguely, you get the feeling you are being told not to ask about it.

For the first days of my shadowing, she'd worked in a window-less room shared with four of her co-workers. They each faced their own wall, and there was enough space in the centre of the room so that their swivel chairs did not collide when they backed away from their desks. They all got along well enough to gossip freely about other workers in other departments, some of whom had their very own offices. They talked about the organization's insurance plan and overtime policies. They talked about emails from their superiors. They occasionally spoke of the hypocrisy they encountered from people higher up in the organization. And they could hear the manager in the adjacent room rise to an audible level while on the phone, saying things like, Yes . . . yes, you can't yell . . . You can't yell at people anymore. It's 2016, I mean '17. I don't care. It's 2017. You can't yell at people anymore.

Victoria never added anything. She listened, she was part of it, but I sensed she also felt above it all. It was daily and repetitive, seemingly enriching because it built a bond among the workers, yet it also seemed to amplify their powerlessness. And though it led nowhere, I couldn't help but feel Victoria was processing it into something bigger. She was listening for something that would be useful to her. She frequently disappeared to the washroom, or to the one window that was not bounded by a desk or office walls. From there we could see the building where I became her shadow. She would look at the building as though processing it too.

Late that first week, Victoria's manager had a visit from someone higher up. The conversation began behind the manager's closed door, but when it seemed to be finishing, after the door had opened, the higher-up kept talking at the door, not making his exit for a good twenty minutes. Though out of view from Victoria's office, we heard him make a few jokes, enthusiastically conveying the state of things, acting as though the world was at ease with itself. Everyone listened in. Finally the conversation ended and, after a pause, he popped his head into our room. This was the first time I had seen him though I'd heard his name mentioned already. The women in the office referred to him as The Beach, because someone had been to his office and there saw a picture of him with his family on a beach, shirt off, chest exposed to sunlight. Even now the impression of his shoulders and the flatness of his stomach was evident through his dress shirt. His name was Said.

Hi everyone.

All the women said, Hi, Said, attentively.

Victoria said hi as well, with professional friendliness.

Oh, hi Victoria, he said. Hi . . . as if wanting to pick up from some recent conversation. When he left, the whole room felt buoyant, even optimistic, for a few minutes.

Victoria typed his name into the Learning Ecologies website, and after his profile came up, followed a link an industry magazine. He appeared on their 'Rising Stars Under 40' page. As a co-worker came by, Victoria closed the page, but I was left with that photo image of the man with his recent haircut and lavender shirt, and with the fact that he was under 40, which was hard for me to believe. Eighty grand a year, I imagined, or ninety or a hundred – it was difficult to voice this, even in my head, without it sounding full of resentment, but there was no resentment there, more wonder at what happens. Money and employment seemed to add years to a face, or give a facial patina won only by those means. And there was something more than all that – the same-age/older-look phenomenon suggested some other state of being, the world having affected him differently, his historical trajectory diverging from my own. A parallel history though we were the same age and lived in the same city.

After Said had left the room that day, one of Victoria's officemates said that he occasionally went by a certain pub after work. Sometimes he met with a friend, another handsome man, who, unlike Said, was likely a bachelor; other times he sat alone with his tablet, probably working overtime on something. Just one drink before getting home to his family. Victoria had taken all this in, as she now goes to the pub after work each day, presumably to accidentally run into him.

I remember another part of Jan Melbrooks' speech one morning as Victoria stands in her condo evaluating a variety of skirt and top combinations. It comes to me as sound without a visual. I can't recall when he spoke it, whether at the beginning or end of his speech, but they were his words, his unwavering vocal style:

For some generations it is the occurrence of an event that allows a zeitgeist to coalesce. Those young people experienced it with their Berlin Wall. Those for whom the 9/11 attacks were a life-changer experienced it. Even those who were simply born in time to witness the millennium turning over know what this feels like. But for others there is no event around which one gains or spends their energy. For them there is just the slow, creeping change that either mimics the feeling of hope or the feeling of dread. They perhaps find a source of energy from somewhere less momentous, even in the most pop-cultural of places. In a movie or music video. No young people can live without this energy and the inherent promise it gives them. The fact that you have all come here today speaks to what is in the air, to something you have all experienced out there in the world, sometime in the past, something that you have latched on to and that speaks beyond yourselves as individuals. Something that you all have decided is yours. I will not say what it is that you have or have not experienced. But it has brought you together to this place.

Something about him I cannot see past. He had shown the enthusiasm, the positivity, the package deal of a lunch-hour speaker, and I had signed up for all he had to offer merely by being present. And I really had been captivated by his speech and overhead images. Everything about him seemed to be about gain rather than loss, even though it should have been clear to anyone that a shadow meant nothing but loss. And yet, I think, observing Victoria put on another skirt in the mirror, these boyishly narrow hips, small breasts, thin legs, these fragmented details that I feel guilt in enumerating come together in a frame that has a kind of perfection to it. She feels like a gain. The only thing that allows all the losses I endured in becoming a shadow, the only gift given to me that makes my shadow-life liveable, even agreeable, is this young female body whose boyish-girlish curves I am condemned to mimic, to lean into, and whose work I have consented to silently absorb.

The **Men's** *Club* generation was the same as my parents' generation, the same as my friends' parents' generation and my teachers' generation. They were all of a generation. And they had made such an overwhelming reality that stretched forward and threw its hands around the present. At least they seemed wrapped around my present. My future reality was somehow embodied in their past experiments in living, but at the same time I felt fully excluded from those experiments. Their story remained an unavoidable and seemingly unchangeable influence over the present.

I realized, perhaps because of *The Men's Club* author and his essay on adapting his novel to film, that work for me was measured by way of that generation. They were a diachronical behemoth, influencing everything that followed. Their work, their tenured professions, their accidenting into lucrative lifelong pursuits. Seemingly there were more right places at the right times than ever before for them. Open doors at every turn. Their trajectories seemed so magnificent.

Always paired with the diachronic was the synchronic, those people my own age, like Etti, like her friend F, like my friends. The synchronic was my generation. I used to be close to so many people who I rarely saw these days. They were all doing things, but their jobs had a random quality to them. No one could have predicted 15 years ago what they would be doing today. Their CVs told a story in bulleted lists and summaries, dated in months and years, but they were not really stories. Yet surely their acts of employment influenced my own.

These two generations – my parents' and my friends' – intersected in me. This is how the diachronic and synchronic worked on a person, locating them at the crossroads of powerful forces, preventing them from being outside of anything. In this abstract way of looking at my life, I became a tiny point on an endless grid.

If I were that point produced by intersecting vectors of my parents' generation and my generation, by my parents' jobs and by my friends' jobs, there must also have been another point somewhere so that my situation could change: a point on the horizon by which I could imagine a movement away from where I was. And if there were indeed such a point, that point would allow a line of reality, a vector of sure motion, beginning with where I stood and continuing outward to the distant point. When I try to picture that line, what it looks like, what it is made of, I see a thin pencil mark across that grid – a perspective line – drawn with a ruler. I see lines of other colours and weights that it crosses or runs parallel to. And because Victoria has again pulled up the 'Under 40' page, I think, perhaps one of those lines is Said's. Victoria's must be there too, parallelling it but at the same time running its own course. What I picture beyond those pencil lines, right now, at this moment in which Victoria is scrolling through the Learning Ecologies website, having put 'job shadowing' into the search engine before deleting it, is nothing. I cannot see anything at all.

After several evenings it finally happens. She waits on a bar stool, sipping a beer and reading a book about self-branding as a business strategy, and he enters. At first she acts as if she doesn't see him, but after he has got the bartender's attention she looks over and their eyes meet.

He joins her, standing tentatively beside her stool as he waits for his drink. They greet each other, and after he pays the bartender and is about to leave she says, Wait, I wanted to ask you about something.

Go ahead, he says.

I have a background in business as well as education. Not many people have that combination, but I see those things as very much informing one another. I mean, I see a lot of potential there. It's kind of my thing, so I'm excited about exploring it further.

And she begins telling him about an idea she has, one she hasn't told her own boss, at least not since I've entered the picture. She says: It's about making students entrepreneurs, but not in a conventional way. My idea would be to have students crowdsource as part of personal branding. Sort of like gathering votes of confidence. And she continues with her idea and asks Said, when she has finished, Do you know what I mean?

Said says, Yes, I think I know what you're saying. But can you give an example?

I don't know. I mean, I purposefully don't know. It would be their decision. Perhaps they would be given a problem, an existing company that they had to compete with. Or an established individual they had to compete with.

Said downs the last of his beer. Victoria has not touched hers.

I would love to head this project, she says, but feel limited in my capacity to get something going at Learning Ecologies. I mean, it feels beyond my job description. I see myself as far more than how my job is defined.

Yes, I know what you mean. Said smiles the whole time. It begins to feel like his default setting. I don't think I can help you there, he says. Maybe I can. People are fairly intent on keeping their jobs secure, as they are. And sometimes that means not opening up possibilities for others. One person moving means other people moving, and not everyone is into that.

I've got ideas. I need to shape my job rather than the other way around. I want to make myself indispensable.

Victoria looks at his hand, its breadth and dark hair.

We should talk again, Said says. Everything else going okay? The job shadowing?

And she answers yes, without hesitation. Yes, of course. I mean I like to keep it to myself. But yes.

That evening after she encounters Said in the bar, she returns to her condo, and before I understand what's going on, she steals me from my analysis of Said, sliding her hand beneath the drawstring of her pyjama bottoms between her legs. She then pulls her hand out, gets up and closes the blinds. I notice a figure in the condo across the gap, a man standing at the window, perhaps noticing us since Victoria's living room is well lit and darkness has fallen outside. Victoria searches through her iPod and lands on what seems to be a movie soundtrack, then returns to the couch and lies back with her earbuds in place. As though to prove how little I am in her consciousness, she simply begins. My hand follows hers through all these simple but precise elliptical motions. I might have put up resistance had shadowing not overcome me so swiftly, had I not been bewitched by the power of a new, foreign body, and the odd freedom of invisibility, so that without hesitation I descend from whatever place I imagined I occupied to the centre of Victoria's motion. I can do nothing but massage along with her. I can do nothing but aim for grace rather than resistance, as if I've had any say whatsoever since I became her shadow.

When she does it again, in bed the next morning, I act as though I'm helping. Now as she makes the same motion in semi-wakefulness, I work to produce an erection out of the shadow of her slender hand. Not that she necessarily wants this, I realize. Maybe at first I assume she wants it. I have no insight, but the effort makes me feel that I am being a better shadow. Perhaps she helps by shaping her hand so that the formed shadow resembles an erection that is then mine. But in mounting frustration she says, "Come on." Something is not working for her. I try harder. I try to conform better to her shape. I have no idea if it does anything. Of course I have no control over myself. Again, "Come on," and again I try to do better, this time working harder on my shape. Then, ineluctably, I'm overcome. There is a release. Just when she seems to be giving up, I feel release.

Etti

The last time she was with F in person was at a big fundraising gala, where a selection of artists were invited to come for free, as attractions of the night - and in one sense they were the whole pretext for the event - while the rest paid at a fundraiser's rate: philanthropists or people who identified themselves with an idea of art viewership and who were desirous to be part of it all. Etti was surprised she'd been invited, and perhaps only when an occasion like this gala came up did she consider what her ranking was among other artists of the city. The pedagogy of her work required time to explain, as did its eventness, that it happened in time and space collaboratively, making it an effort to describe what it looked like, which was at the heart of what people almost always wanted to know. She had been at it for long enough that it was just what she did, it was an extension of her, and others who had followed her work over the years saw a new project just as the next iteration of a series of similar works, one more of her experiments with adolescents doing group work in strange places, or so she likely thought as she glanced around at the big players in the art world who were being celebrated. Her dear friend, standing right beside her, had recently entered the art-world limelight, her name ballooning from the excavations she had made of her ever-more-public sex-life, presenting her findings in a collision of mediums, often everyday objects from her life treated with a jarring arrangement, a crystal-clear reality, smart work propelled to the foreground because sex is always foreground, but also because her variety of honest excavation slipped in amid a present zeitgeist. The work was unadorned and unsentimental except where sentimentality enabled a sense of vulnerability to come through. People were taking it seriously, people were taking F very seriously, and among those doing the vulnerable open sex thing F had risen into visibility while some had remained obscure. Even Etti was likely taking it more seriously now that the timing was right, now that it had become part of what really felt like a historical moment. Somehow its coincidence with the energy of the moment overshadowed all the flaws of the work that might still have remained there. All this to the degree that Etti was starting to think that she herself needed to do more to embrace the current zeitgeist in her own work.

Now they were drinking shoulder to shoulder, tall, thin, attractive in the eyes of benefactors, taking in the people whom they'd never seen before. They talked about feeling like curiosities on display, but also enjoyed the low-level stardom occasions of real money conferred to those typically not looking for it. How fucked up it all was but how that was part of it, and how delving into its fucked-upness gave them a little charge.

A photographer came around and told them to stand close to each other, and they already were, their shoulders touching, and he wanted them even closer. He squatted and then got up and firmly pressed them together with his hands, camera dangling from his neck, before returning to his photographer's stance. Etti stared blankly at the camera and F continued talking while his flash went off in a few rapid white bursts, and he moved on to another cluster of people. Perhaps because it was integral to her work, and perhaps because she enjoyed dressing up and going out, F attended more parties than Etti. Perhaps because she had had a succession of short-term relationships, and in that sense had few commitments, and so was always thinking of the next one, the next art party, whereas Etti had been with Gil for quite some time. And it was from this party experience, Etti supposes, thinking about it on the breezy deck of the superyacht *Nancy*, that F determined she needed to set a goal for every night she went out to one. It took me so long to figure this out, F had said to Etti that night at the contemporary art fundraising ball. I must have been to hundreds of parties, starting in art school, one after the next. Thursdays, Fridays, Saturdays. Some were superfun. We go to parties because we want to be among certain people, after all, so it's natural to be part of that. But then I aged and got tired of them. At some point I looked back at myself at these parties and felt my heart drop. All the parties all the way back to art school. The accumulated effect on me was that parties started having this bad relationship to time. I felt I was wasting time. I can't believe how long it took me to realize this. I mean, it's not that I never felt that I was wasting time before, F had said, it's just that I had been able to blindly disregard it because I was so caught up in the present. I had ignored the boredom of parties, which surely was one of their main qualities. I had said to myself there is no such thing as wasting time because that's what I'd learned in art school. Wasting time is a truism born from capitalism – that was what art school taught us, and the right response was to resist it by not buying into it. But then I realized there was such a thing as wasting time. Since we are stuck in capitalism there is such a thing as wasting time. That is what I realized. So I finally decided, you know, Etti – and Etti wanted to know – I finally decided I needed a goal. Being at parties, merely being present, though essential to my work as an artist, was not enough. I needed a clear focal point that I could aim for over the course of the evening. Even if the evening meant going from one place to another, one opening to another, I needed that visible point. In a sense I needed to imagine a possibility in the party that wasn't otherwise obvious. I needed to speculate on a golden potential that was hidden in the near-future of the party. And in that way I got much deeper into parties.

They gazed at a small group of art-world benefactors, trim suits and trim dresses, chatting in a closed circle. A giant disco ball sent pink and white points of light orbiting across the room, across their faces, the gallery transformed so easily into a dance club. Look at this party, F said. If it's supposed to benefit artists, surely I should have a goal. I should have ten goals, but ones totally unrelated to drinking and dancing.

I don't know, Etti said. Don't you need a break from goals? And at that moment the volume of the party music seemed to double.

Etti didn't ask what the goal for this particular party was, but F did say, shouting in her ear, The goals shouldn't become part of the known, because that adds an extra kind of pressure. It might even work against the goal coming to fruition. I probably shouldn't have even mentioned it to you, the existence of it, but of course I know you won't mention it to anyone. Still, it's out there now – it's beyond my brain and I know it is. You have heard it. It's crossed that crazy distance.

Etti thought about herself at the gallery-benefit party that she didn't really want to be at, though happy to be with F. It's hard to come up with one, she said.

It takes practice, like everything, F said. You need to imagine what you want in the future.

It's easier not to have one, or at least not to think about them as deliberately as that. I mean, it's funny to think that going deeper into a party means having a non-party goal in it. It's like shifting the angle of your presence.

They drifted around the room, running into other friends, and Etti wondered what the goal was, whether F intended to infiltrate the mind of someone who had a lot of money – though that somehow seemed too obvious, and as she started into a conversation with someone else she forgot entirely about F's goal. And if she had been trying to think of one for herself, she dropped that as well, and let the string of party conversations take over. But once an idea entered Etti's head it remained there, became part of the way she thought about the world, and would surface again. What stuck with her in the moment was the fact that F had been living with these goals for so long without telling her about them, when Etti thought she had known her so well. This goal thing was entirely out of the blue. She was not hurt so much as in wonder at the recognition, and with it she altered her mental image of what her friend was, because, after all, she carried a mental version of F around in her mind, one that she dialogued with, bounced ideas off of, made decisions with that affected the course of her own life.

She has been swept up in the *Nancy* party now for hours and hours, beginning on deck where she introduced herself to a group of Caslon's guests, telling them that she'd come across the ocean for the party, before moving on to other people seated at portable aluminum tables. An alien energy has infiltrated her. From the White Nights, she likely imagines, having heard of them but never before experiencing them. The barely dimming sky, a constant twilight, the ceaselessness of day giving her an almost fake kind of energy. She believes it to be real, though, and goes with it.

Etti is the only one in costume in the early afternoon, tattered and re-stitched distress-patterned fabrics wrapped around her forearms and torso, an urchin or hobo costume, a vagrant or travelling performer or something, she never does figure out what it is, though she grows to like it. Nevertheless she is somewhat self-conscious because occasionally a sour odour enters her nose. Like excretions from a street person, someone untethered, urine and sweat and age. She sniffs the air, believing the salt water and the ocean life that surrounds her to be the source, but it clings closer to her, and the ocean water is way down below. Drawing her wrist to her nose she confirms that it's on her, her costume impregnated by it. Nevertheless she keeps the costume on, thinking that it is absolutely essential now, that it would be added alongside the blindfold as documentation of her project. At intervals she gets up and introduces herself to another group of people who don't seem to notice the scent. Food and drinks come by constantly. Hours pass when suddenly so many people have emerged from out of the woodwork, wearing a mix of costumes and high-end dress clothes. There is no sense of exclusivity even though they are way out in the water, gently bobbing in the Bay of Finland on a multi-million dollar superyacht. People pull up by motorboat and others are dropped off by a helicopter. She wonders why she was forced to wear the blindfold when so many others seemed to arrive so freely, but the thought passes, since Etti is caught up in it all. Everyone is in high spirits. The deck of the *Nancy* transforms into a street festival, the air buzzing with the desires of this small pocket of humanity.

Early that evening she begins speaking with a man who calls himself an architect. He puts his hand on her elbow and forearm and smiles a lot, asking her to tell him more about herself. His first name is the same as a famous architect and she wonders whether that famous architect is in fact the very man she is talking to. Many people have the name Igor, she thinks at the time. If she'd had her phone she might have done an image-search of the architect just to confirm. That is the mood she is in, a mood that makes her want to know a detail like that, one in which some satisfaction would be derived from knowing and from matching a real-life man to screen image. But more: encountering a famous person gives the feeling that a door might be opened, an opportunity might emerge from out of the wealth or power, and that such an opportunity can be capitalized on, or so she likely considers since that is her frame of mind as she listens to the possibly famous man.

The architect is dressed as a fish, a tight-fitting costume that shows off his body. His teeth are perfectly white but a little crooked. His face is masked from nose up in iridescent scales. What are you doing on board? she keeps meaning to ask, but instead listens to the man. The other night he had been to a Soviet-themed bar in Helsinki owned by Finland's most famous director, Aki Kaurismäki. That was fun, he says. Next door is another bar owned by Kaurismäki, he continues, a pool bar where I went afterwards. It was there that I saw a picture that really hit me. It hit me with a great force, he says. In that second bar was a framed print of a man. He had this moustache, it was a leaden moustache, and greasy hair that was parted in the middle. A three-quarter turn to the camera – and here the architect shifts in relation to Etti to become the picture he is describing – a suit jacket over white T-shirt and kerchief tied around his neck, making him look sweet despite everything else. Despite being dishevelled, I mean, because he looked defeated by the world, says the architect. His gaze was emptied of personal interest, drained of ambition, and trailed off past the photographer, as if the room went on and on and on into nothingness. I had to ask the bartender his name. That is Matti Pellonpää, he said. Matti Pellonpää. In the picture he looked like there was nothing left in him. And in fact there is nothing left of him, the architect says. He is dead. Several years dead now. The bartender told me that Pellonpää lived without an apartment and would borrow clothes from the people whose apartments he slept in. I guess he owned nothing. And in that way his life was almost indistinguishable from those slow, bleak

69

films he appeared in. When I got home to my hotel room that night I watched one of them on my laptop. I couldn't sleep with the White Nights and the drinking and all the hours of talking at the bar. Have you seen *La Vie de Bohème*? It's on YouTube.

No, she says. I don't know it. Etti is feeling indifferent about their conversation, half-listening to the architect, wondering about his fame, and letting go of that desire in order to half-listen to herself and especially to the idea that she has intended on carrying through with: to talk to people and to value their opinions above that version of F that she carries in her head, her thinking being that that version of F is just a version, a mental construct. And one step beyond that, she also tries now to value the opinion of the people she meets above her own opinions. She's not sure about the latter, though she wonders if what she's read about valuing other people's opinions is the same as what she remembers reading, and wonders if the person who wrote it was taking a radical position for the sake of it, or maybe theorizing a distant position without actually meaning that someone go about life that way, valuing others' opinions above one's own. It seems crazy to her, right now, to value the architect's opinion above her own, even though he has offered very few opinions.

Pellonpää plays Rodolfo, the architect continues, a painter from Albania struggling to make a living from his work. In his first scene he sits in an empty Parisian restaurant with a plate of trout – and Etti recognizes that the architect himself may be dressed as a trout. A playwright comes in after Rodolfo and seats himself, orders two half-trouts, but is informed by the waiter that they're out of trout. Rodolfo, it turns out, has the last one. Rather than keeping it to himself, though, Rodolfo offers to share his trout, which happens to be a two-headed trout, and they eat the trout together, becoming fast friends. Rodolfo is helplessly generous.

Though he goes on without a break, the architect maintains gentle eye contact with Etti, showing concern for the viability of their conversation. She in turn watches his eyes under the awkward mask, and they seem familiar to her. She considers asking to see his face, but doesn't want to interrupt him. As he finishes describing the plot of *La Vie de Bohème*, he says, That photograph, the defeated one in Kaurismäki's pool bar, is from that movie. Of course, despite being like the characters he portrays, he is never them. I don't believe in such transferability. Though he lived like a bohemian in a way that almost no one does, especially now, he was not the bohemian Rodolfo. No one can be two people. But even though I believe this – I'm fully behind the idea of non-transferability – I couldn't help but say yes to the bartender when he said that that picture *was* him, Pellonpää *was* Rodolfo. He said that Pellonpää would share a two-headed trout with a complete stranger. I find that to be fascinating though I know it's just pure fantasy.

The architect pauses, allowing Etti to speak, but she remains silent.

Later that night I played pool with Caslon in that bar, the architect says. It was dark and empty at the time. Somehow I already knew that he was a huge fan of *La Vie de Bohème*. Maybe he hadn't even seen it yet, but he would. It's one of his favourites now. I think he likes it so much because he relates to Rodolfo. I mean at some level. Not the poverty, but there is something so appealing to him in that life. You've met Caslon?

Yes, Etti says. I don't know much about him though. I didn't know he was into film. How did you meet him?

Oh. I can't recall exactly where it was. I suppose I haven't known him for very long. I feel as though I've known him forever, though. We share so much in common.

And then the architect asks her about her art practice, and he begins with his 'tell me more,' and each project that she describes needs more explanation. He can't get enough of her, and he laughs and touches her forearm when she jokes about the lack of wisdom of teenagers – perceptive but completely unwise, she says – and again when she jokes about living in unpleasant places, and again when she tells him about the coffee that she was supposed to buy for the gas station convenience store clerk – which seems like weeks ago or part of some other dimension of time even though it was that very morning – and then, having felt his touch seek something more from her, says, Please excuse me, I need to find a washroom.

Of course, he says. I'll look out for you later. I'd like to talk with you more. I mean, how is it that you've ended up at this party in the first place? Did Caslon just meet you on land?

Etti is not far enough away to avoid answering. Yes, she says, I just met him. He brought me here. But we corresponded before meeting. And the fish architect smiles as she turns away and disappears through the crowd of partyers.

72

Thereafter she actively avoids the fish architect, engaging with some of the other partyers, hiding behind groups. She follows a couple she has just met down a wide staircase, and the couple step away as soon as they reach the door to a games room, assimilating into a loud, intoxicated tableau inside, leaving Etti to enter by herself. She pauses before squeezing through to the opposite end, where she takes a seat beside a young woman. Though the woman is sitting alone on the couch she feels no pressure to talk. They make eye contact but say nothing to one another. And there on the couch perpendicular to hers sits Caslon. The encounter feels inevitable to her. She sees him as himself, no costume on.

He holds a controller in the direction of a massive flat screen TV, pausing a football match and using the controller to zoom in so that the screen is filled with the head and shoulders of two players. Then he releases the pause and the image proceeds in super-slow motion. It is clear, fairly quickly, even before the collision, that the player in white will head-butt the player in blue, and Etti recognizes the blow, remembering the name of the one player, the head-butter, to be Zidane. She's seen art pieces made about the Algerian-French player and this defining moment from the 2006 World Cup final.

She looks over to Caslon to try to understand what this is all about, and he is fixated on the image, joyfully living it out.

Maybe it's this she was searching for: that taking another person's opinion above our own is valuable because our thoughts

– the place where real thinking takes place – only happen at the edge of our thoughts, new thoughts only happen at the edge of what we already know, and since the other's thoughts are already outside our thoughts, they offer a road beyond our own. And even if the other's thoughts are so far outside of our own that we can barely recognize them, at least they create a territory of newness between ours and theirs. Perhaps this is what the author had written, though she is not at all sure now. And she has surely forgotten any qualifications the author made to the proposition.

Clearly Caslon's been holding court, and Etti has entered at the critical point when he comes to the statement he'd been working towards. And it does come. Zidane's head-butt, he says, was our generation's moon landing – that's just how different our generations are.

She absorbs what he is saying while her brain conflates the roundness of Zidane's shaved head with the World Cup soccer ball and a black and white moon image. Caslon glances around to those people caught up in his gravitational field, standing and drinking, and they are mostly younger than him. Though some are in costumes, what she is able to see are people in their twenties. They don't react to his statement. He wasn't speaking to them at all really, not when he said 'our generation.' Certainly not when he named the moon-landing generation. Only Etti herself is roughly the same age as Caslon, hovering near forty.

There must be more to a generation than simply a date of birth, she thinks, because people of the same age often look upon one another as though alien beings. Some people of Etti's so-called generation would never have heard of Zidane and therefore never had his actions affect their worldview, which is surely what Caslon is implying with his comparison to the moon landing. And though she herself *has* seen the head-butt, she is fairly certain that her worldview has not been affected by it, that there was no paradigm shift that threw a rope around her and others. Caslon's statement, rather than inviting her to his circle of experience, makes her feel excluded from it, part of something else entirely.

A server comes around with a tray of drinks, and she takes one. She recognizes the next song that comes on. The cluttered games room washes over her, testing her mental stamina. At times she knows she is not powerful enough to ward off the on-slaught of sensory stimuli. No space, she is likely thinking. This place in all of its partyness is overdetermined. She wants either to get up and dance or escape to her quarters.

When Caslon speaks again, he faces her. He addresses her directly. Because, he says, they were caught up in accomplishing a fantastic idea, one that people had imagined for centuries and one towards which so much energy and money and research was thrown. One that was especially timely as part of a global competition – taking the moon. By stark contrast, we are caught up in the thing that no one imagined but that, once done, retrospectively seems so inevitable that it *not* happening would then seem an impossibility. Toward which we feel, when it happens, What!? Impossible! before saying, Of course, that had to happen! They imagined a future in which there would be social relations on the moon, perhaps including East–West friendships. Their very horizon had been extended beyond reason, whereas we have given up our future-feeling in order to embrace the present as inevitable even when its events are unforeseeable. Zidane simply revealed what was always in view but which no one would acknowledge. A football match is never just a football match. Imagine all the forces at play.

His voice carries over the music and partyers, holding the attention of those surrounding him. He has focused on Etti. She has come across the Atlantic for him and now that he's making declarations she feels obliged to begin her work, to record him.

Etti, he yells, and pats the sofa cushion beside him. Come.

After she has sat down, he says, Watch this. He lets the famous headbutt to the chest run in super-slow motion, revealing every shift in emotional state on their faces, tanned skin tightening and slackening, every muscle of Zidane readying for collision. The emergent dumbfoundedness on the Italian player's face. Look at them, he says, their mouths and cheeks and brows, the creases in their skin. Look how ugly even this most beautiful of men is when we can see the slightest shifts in his expression, his facial muscles marshalling the violence of his reaction. This view is too much, isn't it. This is what people are, though we never see them like this.

Etti watches. She has seen the head-butt before but not in as much detail and never with someone urging her in this way. It is a fascinating image. The superyacht party makes it delirious.

This is art, isn't it, he says to Etti. Etti continues watching.

Zinedine Zidane, the artist disruptor, destroying the purity of the beautiful game, he continues. But this is old now just like the moon landing. It has done its job. And Caslon looks to Etti as though for confirmation.

You know, Etti, he says loudly enough for everyone around them to hear, you were not my first choice for this. After I got your proposal I contacted a number of other people. I liked your idea but thought you were not the person to execute it. So I phoned Lars von Trier. I've always admired his view of life. Then Leos Carax, the French director. Pedro Costa, the Portuguese director. I was thinking it could be a film and their films feel very real to me. But I kept searching. I asked myself, who is the world's most pure thinker? I contacted Murakami. I contacted Pynchon. I'm not sure why I contacted those two. I didn't really want them, but I wanted to contact them. I contacted Jean-Philippe Toussaint. And Michel Houellebecq. And Alexander Kluge. Peter Handke. Men men men, you are probably thinking. That was okay with me, but they are past their prime. Most importantly, the clarity that marked their earlier work is disappearing. I contacted a Russian poet named Skidan. I contacted Lisa Robertson, the Canadian. I contacted the comedian Aziz Ansari. My idea for the project kept changing with each person I thought of. I went through the list of TED Talks speakers – photographers, technology people, so-called visionaries in their fields. I contacted Nadezhda Tolokonnikova of Pussy Riot, but she would not respond. Of course I wanted her to do it. Then I thought there should be some artists in the mix. I love to throw money at artists. And artists are so often the only ones who have the sense of freedom I decided I was looking for. I thought and thought of someone whose brain was like a prism that could either focus light to a single intense point or, tilted, stratify it into its constitutive colours. Someone whose vision could scalpel through all of the stuff of the present. Someone young, who could shift the way reality is represented, and whose boldness was not yet weighed down by the world. But I am happy that all of them said no. They had their various reasons. I'm happy it is you that came. Not just because it was your idea – though ideas are often best carried out by the people who came up with them. It is more than that. Look at you, you are perfect for this. You are the perfect writer of my life.

And without a pause, he gets up and commands the room's attention with a sweeping gesture. Everyone, he says, this is Etti. Please welcome her to the *Nancy*. And he disappears into one of the corridors of the yacht.

She wakes the next day in a strange bed, in a room full of things that are not hers, and everything seems simplified. She has no obligation other than to the project. The yacht keeps the rest of the world away. It is isolated.

Still, she desires to begin defining things, knowing that defining some things means excluding most others. A cutting away of most of the world in order to beam a light of clarity on a slice of it. In a sense the whole world is a fucked-up state until she chooses to cut away most of it. Art is the act of exclusion. The goal of art is to exclude, she thinks at this particular moment, from her small bed on the superyacht.

She thinks: every goal involves some other person. That is the key that is often overlooked. Even a goal that proposes to improve the individual life, to better the self, whether through exercise or classes or a simpler or slower lifestyle, others come into the picture, teachers and coaches and friends, and when it comes to work, to employment, those people are not necessarily interested in helping. There is no way to get around it. Not that Etti wants to get around it. Most goals, she gets to thinking, most don't just involve other people. Most require paying other people, and some require convincing or manipulating other people. Most involve wedging oneself into new situations that demand a response from others. She hopes that whatever happens with Caslon will demand as little manipulation as possible. She hopes they can figure out a place of equal ground.

It is early afternoon, and she leaves her room and heads to the deck, not really knowing where else to go. There are no signs that the party has happened. The tables are gone, the wood is clean and dry, the sun is beating down. The people have all disappeared. It feels remote, empty.

She takes a chair and reclines and closes her eyes against the sun, as though that might be her first exclusion.

When she opens them, the man in white is standing above her. Nelson, she says.

Can I get you anything?

No, I don't think so. Do you know where we're going?

I can't say.

Oh, she says. Do you mean that you don't know or that you are not allowed to say?

The yacht is not moving at all, he says.

Oh, she says, and closes her eyes again. All this time she's pictured it moving.

Anytime, she expects a message from Caslon asking her to come and meet him. The first day goes by, and the second. She decides not to be bothered if she doesn't receive a message on the third day, but feels untethered, having no routine through which to experience the yacht. She hates to face the yacht in a purposeless way, because everything seems just excessive and fucked up but not in an interesting way. It makes her feel like a tourist. She thinks of F, but F would not come to her.

Nelson accompanies her everywhere, not speaking to her unless she speaks to him, smiles but says nothing. He doesn't prevent her from going down any passages or opening any doors, not that she opens many, as all the rooms are labelled with engraved metal signs indicating their purpose. Etti and Nelson frequently pass other employees and what must be other guests, but she doesn't talk to any of them.

On one of her explorations she discovers a wide, empty hallway. From one end to the other runs an aluminum plaque, marked with three lines of text, each line readable only by walking its length back and forth:

SUPERYACHT *IMMANENCE* – *"NANCY"* – DESIGNED IN 2010 BY IGOR WANDERLEI FOR CASLON A. F. MAXIM. BUILT BY TOFFLER & YANOV. MAIDEN VOYAGE MAY 2014.

She does the back and forth, feeling along the sharp metal letters until realizing that she had read somewhere that Igor Wanderlei, the famous architect she'd been thinking of, had died, and that, therefore, the fish man she spoke with at the party could not have been him. In the moment she simply sighs.

In the middle of the third night she is awoken by something. Perhaps a thought she is having. Maybe her mind is sifting through whatever real reasons she might have for being on board the *Nancy*. What does she hope to get from this? she wonders. What does she want from Caslon? And she answers to herself: a project. Something unlike her usual work. And she realizes that each time she imagines what that project might be, she pictures F and her recent success.

She decides she must get out of her room, in full knowledge that whenever she opens the door a buzzer or a light or something must go off somewhere in the yacht, wherever Nelson is, to alert him to her movement. Every time she leaves her room he shows up within a minute, and from this she supposes that his room must be very close to hers. She wonders if there is any way to disconnect this alarm mechanism, which might be triggered by her hand, her fingerprints read by the doorknob. Right now she doesn't worry about it. She opens the door and leaves her room, wearing pyjamas and slippers, and a shawl over her shoulders.

Etti takes the route on deck that she is now used to taking, checking over her shoulder for his appearance. But this time, for whatever reason, he does not appear by her side. She goes along a couple of corridors and up the wide central staircase. No one is around on deck-level, but she knows that someone must be awake on the yacht at all times. A captain or first mate or someone.

Even while she leans against the railing, lost in the black water that washes against the hull way down below, the ideal image of contentment, she becomes impatient. In Caslon's absence she has become antsy.

You know these moments of stasis, F says, are in fact just slack threads that can, and will, snap in a single action, and that that action could come from anyone at any time. Yes, she thinks. You are right, F. There are things to do in this space that I won't be able to do later. And she recognizes that she's been thinking about the plaque, wanting to record it, but has no device with a camera since her phone was confiscated. She returns to her room and takes her sketchbook and carefully tears out sheet after sheet of paper, maybe sixty or so, no doubt trying to recall exactly how large the plaque is, how many sheets she will need, and locates a soft pencil and leaves the room again.

At the end of a hall she sees a sliver of light – an open door –

and hears low sounds seeping out of it. Drawn to these nocturnal hints of life she approaches the door and looks inside. Two men stand face to face in the middle of a hushed argument. The men look identical, both appearing to be Caslon. You stupid, incompetent fuck! says the one. And the other, You fascinating fucking tyrant, and the first, I'm going to fucking . . . you need to get off your fucking ass, and the other, Go ahead, fucknuts, and the first, For fuck's sake do I have to babysit you, and the other, You mean microfuckingmanage me, and the first, Oh, for Christ's sake, you deserve more than this, and with that the first wallops the other across the face with a smartphone, which happens to ring on impact. Etti retreats, hearing the phone skid across the floor and continue to ring. When she looks up she sees Nelson a short way down the corridor. He gives away no reaction to what he must also hear. Rather than heading back to her room she retraces her steps past the door where Caslon and his double are fighting, and toward her previous goal.

The plaque is mostly as she remembers, though now she sees that it is constructed of several panels rather than a single sheet of metal, and what she thought at first to be aluminum seems to be highly polished, mirror-like stainless steel. She holds up a sheet and presses it into the metal to make an impression and then puts the paper aside. With a clean sheet she now covers the first several letters, leaving a little space so that the words are close to the edge but not so tight as to make the rubbing sloppy. She presses her index finger against the pencil's carbon, pushing into the paper, and moves it back and forth, aiming for even coverage and even greyness. The first letter, the S, is almost complete when the pencil lead snaps. It remains in the wooden sheath of the pencil, and she continues to use it until it crumbles into nothingness, then peels back the wood as far as it will go with her thumbnail and continues to rub so that the edges of the letters come into visibility darker than the surrounding grey. SUPERYACHT *IM*. And the pencil is too worn down and she can't peel back at the wood any more with her nail. She sees Nelson against the dullness of the corridor wall. Do you have a knife on you? she asks. He pulls out a restaurant-style corkscrew with a foldable blade, which he opens and hands to her, then steps back. She carves away at the wood until she has a nice nub of carbon, puts the tool in her back pocket, and returns to her rubbing. After each sheet is filled, she places it on the ground below its metal original. She continues for one or two hours until the darkened sheets line the floor the length of the sign. She collects the sheets, placing one on top of the next so that the rubbings don't wear against each other and obliterate the words.

It is likely that focusing on this repetitive task has shielded her thoughts from the two Caslons. There's no room for thinking about the Caslons while she is working, no room for something so complex as two men who appear to be the same person struggling for an unknown reason, yet struggling, perhaps, in the way that any number of other combinations of people might struggle, like brothers or old friends, or maybe like a mentor and pupil. Having spent years now with her modular teen projects, she is rusty with a pencil or a pen, out of practice with drawing, and she notices, in all likelihood, the change in quality of her rubbing from when she begins to when she ends, the final sheets having a lighter yet more precise quality even as her arm was tiring and wrist cramping from the constant controlled motion.

She sits by the pile of paper and looks up at the long plaque. The fish architect had looked like Caslon, and it occurs to her, putting two and two together, that it may well have been a second Caslon who went on so affectionately about Pellonpää while stroking her arm.

When she returns to her room she places the rubbings in the same drawer as her silver blindfold and pauper costume. Even though she has the costume wrapped in a plastic bag, its smell is more potent than ever. It makes her feel nauseous.

Steadying herself against the footboard of her bed, she recognizes what had roused her from sleep: not her own self-questioning at all, but the massive vessel she is on. Because the superyacht, she senses from her feet, from her head and guts, is moving. It unsettles her now that it is really happening, now that someone has determined one direction against all possible directions. She sits on the edge of her bed, taking deep breaths. This is the fact of a yacht, she says to herself. The anchor comes up. The whole thing moves, and with it so does everyone on board, and in that it is not just unsettling, but also maybe galvanizing.

Victoria

Late in my education, I engaged with an ideal buried in the longest book I ever read. In the novel there are dozens of characters, innumerable names on the page, some off to the margins, isolated, and some freely intersecting, their stories intricately interwoven into a web of human life. The main character, named Mayne, imagines he is reunited with his ex-wife. Already he carries on intermittent psychic communications with her, well past the date of their separation. But then he takes it further. In his fantasy their physical reunion begins on a metal plate somewhere on earth - they meet there - and then they are sent into the space outside the earth's atmosphere where they meld into a single being. Something miraculous transpires, bringing them in a single consciousness out there on the moon or firmament or wherever the author sets them. In the world of the novel, this fusion of souls is our human outcome. It is our destiny. I don't remember what happens to them next, what happens after the lunar coupling. Perhaps the author wrote what happens next, but it is likely that there was nowhere to go from there. The fantasy ends. It is left as an image, as is, as a bewildering end goal.

Victoria discreetly, quietly as possible, dashes past seated co-workers down the hall to the washroom where she finds an open stall and leans into the toilet bowl. When the same thing happened that night of her birthday, with the vodka and cupcakes, it was a little jolt to me, physically I felt her lurch, and it was unpleasant to be abandoned to someone's poisonous throes. But I didn't think much of it. I didn't wonder why she was throwing up. I likely would have done the same with the flavoured alcohol accumulating in my stomach. But now she was throwing up midway through the morning for no obvious reason. She hadn't been out the night before. She'd eaten very little for breakfast. She'd simply been at her desk sending emails, copying and pasting names into an Excel spreadsheet. It must have come on quickly. She throws up a little bit of food and heaves a little more, producing a weak dribble she has to spit to release. She avoids clinging to the seat as they do in movies, instead hugging herself as her chin moves forward, then crouches away from the toilet and waits.

She must have an inner life like everyone, but her look in the mirror, after cleaning herself up, tells me nothing of what is going on in there. That inner life with anxieties and desires and fantasies that remains hidden from the world, however much those same anxieties are shared by others. Especially those of people like her co-workers, I think, because surely anxieties are common among people. But what eats away at her generation, I can only guess at. I can read nothing of it from her daily actions. I watch and listen, but she lets on so little.

She composes herself and re-enters the office, and no one seems to have noticed her dash to the bathroom. I follow as I always do, and she works with her usual focus until 5:10 p.m.

Those who came of age in the '60s and '70s had imagined that the orgasm enabled a unity of souls. Orgasms of oneness, at least the attainment of something as close to oneness that we would ever achieve. That spurting and shuddering and gasping threw a metaphysical coil around two people, winding tightly around them so that the lovers lost themselves at the instant they became one. It was such a beautiful solution. How could one not believe in it? And divorced as it was from the anxiety of reproduction – the introduction of a third person, a baby, into the equation – it was a perfect end in and of itself, complete and unburdened. Clear-sighted, a true destination.

With Victoria and I, one half of the couple remains flesh and blood, lithe and vital, and the other remains shadow. One has a job and lives her life unhappily bound to the job while the other gives up his identity and habits to become a drab and flat observer of someone else's preoccupations. But there is no denying that we are one, that this is a version of oneness, and that it is not the same as the orgasm version, and that this is not what they had imagined in the '60s and '70s.

Perhaps, I think, now at Victoria's condo, watching her compose an email that would go out to schools and parents after channelling through her supervisor and the Ecologies copy editor, this is the exact aim of humanity, one person losing his life blood so that another knows where she stands. Or hers for his. The sexes don't matter, so long as there is an absolute imbalance. One quietly observes while the other earns, assembling her life through objects bought both at discount and at high-end stores. One shadows excursions to New York and Mexico and Southeast Asia, and sits back at dinners of southern barbeque and tacos and ramen and Napolese pizza. One watches her rom-coms and serialized television intended for teenagers. One watches the other compose her life story more or less as she chooses, or as much as anyone chooses, while kicking back into one's own grey nothingness.

Normally she would go to the gym around this time of the evening, then have a light dinner, and I can only imagine that she is still not feeling well, that perhaps she has picked up the flu or something, and that I will have to suffer through it with her.

She goes to bed early but cannot sleep, so she takes a book from her side table. At times she closes it to look at the cover, which is plain white save a shiny ball bearing at its centre. After she opens and closes the book a number of times, I notice that the ball bearing has a little rust spot on it that is barely perceptible. But I doubt she keeps closing the book to return to this image. More likely it is the subtitle of the book, *The Story of Success*, that she wants to see again, or perhaps the reviewer's blurb or the 'millions sold' line. She stares at it as though it will confirm something that the book itself is not revealing, then opens the book again to the page she was reading. She skips ahead when there are charts full of numbers, or when she is bored by something, and I am thankful that she does. Not only are the ideas so simple that any chapter could have been summarized in a couple of sentences, without any loss of nuance, but the author crosscuts between different stories, some violent and some sensationalist – like the last moments of a passenger plane's flight captured on the cockpit voice recorder before it all crashes – in order to create tension, and I get tired of his manipulations. He writes as if his readers are children, telling them what to think at any and every possible moment when they might think for themselves. And somehow this infantilization is worse for me than being a young woman's shadow, making me more depressed than being the shadow. In fact, I really have not been depressed in my time with Victoria. After all, Victoria doesn't tell me what to think. She acts as if I do not exist. Perhaps there is something special in that.

She keeps reading, following the anecdotes about how various people became successful. I wonder if she relates to the author's idea of being an anomaly or whether she just likes to read the stories he uses to exemplify his ideas. Over the weeks since she started, she has arrived at chapters about cultural legacy, where the author suggests how our particular forebears from generations ago lived their lives and how those lives affected our own present worldviews, and more importantly, the likelihood of us succeeding or not. Following the author's logic, I wonder if that means that *their* forebears affected their own successes, all the way back to the original forebear who decided to settle in one place or keep moving on from mountain to valley to shore in search of the best living conditions. And then

I wonder if the original forebear had impossible foresight, and was able to determine which situation would play out best for his offspring and theirs and theirs all the way through history to its very end. While Victoria must know what her parents do for a living, she probably has no idea what her family did 150 years ago, and thus would never come to believe that her employment opportunities of the present were dependent on the kind of farming her great-great-great-grandparents practiced. For my part I have no idea what men and women in my family were doing 150 years ago, never mind whether their lives were determined by decisions from their great-great-great-grandparents. No one can see like that into the future, I think. But I'm also sure that no one can see into the past like this author does.

Before turning out the light, Victoria checks her temperature with an oral thermometer. It is normal. She washes a Tylenol down with a large glass of water before laying on her side, and I am there with her as she turns out the light.

At lunchtime the next day, Victoria gets up from her desk and walks through a door at the far end of the office, one she has not gone through since I joined her. A corridor opens up and she continues through doors and offices, passing cubicles occupied with people I've never seen before. Through a metal door she enters a stairwell that for some reason is in complete darkness. She flips a switch seemingly without thinking and goes up a level, and takes another heavy door out into a corridor and past other doors, at one point backtracking and taking another corridor, this one a skywalk, windowed from end to end on both sides and overlooking the spread of parking lots and beyond to other complexes in their dark browns and vibrant greens. Despite the cars and flat buildings and sloped lawns, there is a surprising beauty to the view. Finally she comes to a long narrow room banked on one side by windows, with several small tables set in a row, the smell of microwaved lunches in the air. At one table sit a woman and the man I recognize as Said. He sees her immediately. Victoria, come join us, he says, and waves her over.

The woman introduces herself and mentions her title at Ecologies. She is much higher up than Victoria. After a pause, the woman asks how long Victoria has been with the organization and if she likes it here. She's in her forties, established, empowered. She seems intelligent.

Victoria says, Well, I'm enjoying it.

Yes, it's a good organization to work for, isn't it?

It *is* a good organization to be with. Yes, of course. I mean one always has to do menial tasks at work, and one starts at a lower level.

Well yes. That's the way it goes, isn't it? So long as you enjoy yourself.

Of course.

Said smiles though says nothing.

Do you enjoy *your* work? Victoria asks the woman.

Why, absolutely.

What is it you like about it?

Well, many things. I feel that what I do positively impacts other people's lives.

As though to help the conversation continue, Said asks Victoria what project she's involved in.

I have ideas for outreach, but they are somewhat beyond my job description.

Oh, but I'm sure your supervisor would like to hear about them, says the woman.

Yes, I've tried to bring them up. The timing seems to be bad.

And the conversation goes on like this, in brief exchanges. Victoria remains poised and she stays with them even after she has finished her lunch. She is waiting for something.

The woman gets up and nods goodbye, saying it was nice to meet Victoria.

When she has left, Said asks Victoria if anything is wrong. He says she looks pale. Oh, I'm fine, she says. Maybe working too hard. He holds her gaze, unsatisfied with her response.

I'd like to meet with you sometime to talk more about my ideas, she says.

I'd like to help, but I don't think I can do anything for you in that respect. If any more opportunities come up that I think you'd benefit from, I'll let you know.

A postcard arrives through Victoria's work mail. The picture side, held in her small, manicured hand, shows five separate views of another era: children playing in a campground sandbox, a rural man herding a flock of sheep, a woman pedalling to work on a quiet street, a passenger train brushing through banks of evergreens, a woman arcing mid-dive above a swimming pool. In the centre is a white rectangle framing the words 'EEN VAKANTIE.' At first I think 'A Vacancy,' then imagine it to mean 'On Vacation.' It is like a vacation for my eyes. I'm taken elsewhere, to another era – a European version of my parents' generation. I believe that the woman really exists, pedalling to work on a quiet street. I believe in that train and the corridor of spruce or fir. I believe in the healthy folks executing clean dives at the pool, and the joy of the sandbox kids and the respectable stoicism of a shepherd caring for his sheep. I'm so willing to believe in this world. Victoria flips the card to look at the message. It is addressed to me, with the Classplaza address on it. *Dear Gil, I might be longer than expected . . .* I catch before she flips the card back over to the picture side. She pins the card up on the office divider above her desk, which is otherwise blank since she hasn't put up any photos since the shuffle. She stares at the board, at the single postcard, and I notice a

94

crease running up the centre where it has been deliberately folded and unfolded. Victoria then takes it down and pushes the swivel chair away from the desk. She puts the card in her back pocket and leaves.

In the washroom something changes. She pushes through the door and listens for other people. She chooses a stall, stands above the toilet, looking down into the basin of water, leans a little forward, hands on thighs. She takes a number of deep breaths before turning and sitting, pants pulled down, on the seat. She just sits. More deep deliberate breaths. She finds the postcard again but keeps it picture side up.

She hunches over, face in hands. The dryer in the adjacent men's washroom goes and I can hear the door close. Standing again, she pulls her pants up and leaves the stall for the sinks. In the mirror is a young woman and no one else. She examines herself, then inspects the tiled floor. The lighting is terrible. She looks up at the translucent screen covering the fluorescent tubes, its molded diamond pattern. Then she begins moving herself slowly in relation to the ceiling light, and looks to the floor again, then back to the boxed fluorescent tubes, then to the floor. She shuffles in place with her head low and turning like a cat confused by its tail. I'm nothing more than a thin fog on the tiled floor, no matter where she stands or how she moves.

I once read that the mirror phase happens early in childhood, around six months. The shadow phase, on the other hand, in which a child is able to predict where their shadow will fall in relation to a light source, happens much later, around age nine. Though no child or infant, Victoria seems suspended between phases, between mirroring and shadowing. And yet, childlike, animal-like, she does this self-conscious modern dance, triangulating between the mirror, the ceiling light, and the washroom floor, and as though to nail down her singularity, she stops herself and pushes the postcard through the swinging top of the garbage can.

It is not as before, that night, when she puts her hand down the front of her pants. Nothing is stimulated by her touch, more she is examining herself, searching for a thing that shouldn't be there. Tears form, then she wipes her sleeve against her forehead and continues to sob. She retreats to her bedroom and curls up under the duvet.

The alarm sounds the next morning and she stays in bed. She phones work and tells them she's under the weather, she won't be in today. But after a while she gets her things together and heads to Learning Ecologies. Her co-workers, one after the next, mention that she doesn't look well but she insists she's okay. She pushes through the day, snacking on rice crackers and sipping water.

For several days she persists in going to work, seemingly against what her body is telling her. Somehow she maintains her duties. She says very little to her co-workers and uses the washroom with the least traffic, where she throws up or splashes water on her face.

Then one day she doesn't make it out of bed. She emails work and says she won't be in today, that she is very sorry and will work from home. From bed she keeps up with her work emails, orders in food and has difficulty getting to the door to pay. Her routine forms quickly, outlined by emailing and other tasks for work, and filled in by watching movies, rom coms and serial television in bed. Partway through episodes she checks her work email, answering questions and keeping up a conversation with her manager, who, while seeming concerned for Victoria's health, never suggests taking a break.

The days go by. One evening, after the final episode of a TV series ends, a movie automatically streams. It begins, but the screen is black. Symphonic music eases out of her laptop's speaker, then builds though there is nothing to see but Victoria's own reflection in the screen. She stares either at the nothingness or at her dark face as the music rises, and then the first shot comes on: the sun rising from behind the earth. The movie cuts to another sunrise, this time the sun edging over the top of a perfectly smooth monolith. Apes enter the scene, and she keeps watching, and they become violent, learning to use a bone as a deadly club, enacting the dawn of man. Everything progresses slowly but inevitably, one large ape emerging as the clear leader of the other apes, and as though to show everyone else what it really means to be him, their leader, he hurls the bone into the air in a fit of ape ecstacy. The film cuts across time and space, the bone becoming a spacecraft drifting against the black vacuum before traversing a spherical backdrop that must be earth. Victoria is lulled into what must be a very deep sleep, but I keep watching. The two spacemen that emerge as central characters begin to doubt their relationship with the ship's computer, how they both depend on it but lose their trust in it, and how the mild computer voice attempts to sway the one man even after it has sent the other to his outer-spatial grave.

I do not want to let that point on the horizon go, I think as I watch the disjointed final sequences of the film, the main character aging alone in palatial rooms. I am lost without that point, however fantastic it ultimately is. And that second point – not the one on the horizon but the one that located me at the intersection of my friends' work and my parents' work – that one no longer applies. Because if that point represented me as an employed human, I am at best the shadow of another point. I am no longer on that gridded plain where such an intersection could exist, but below it somewhere. And if there is no plain below the employed plain, then surely I am nowhere at all. That face reflected in the computer monitor – that is the only point. Victoria's sleeping face, however close or distant it is.

Every time the phone rings, a few feet from Victoria's head, she glances at it, perhaps with dread, then lets it buzz with its new text message. Finally, after someone persists in calling several times in a row, she picks up.

What's going on? the man says. It's Said.

What do you mean?

You haven't been answering the phone.

There is something wrong with me, Victoria says. Something is wrong. I'm not getting any better. I don't get it. I think I'm getting better and then two hours later I'm shit again. I wake up in the middle of the night with awful sweats. I drench the sheets. I don't know what the fuck is wrong.

There is silence on the other end. I should come over.

No, don't.

You've been throwing up?

I feel nauseous all the time. I'm throwing up. It's awful. I can't go to work. I mean, I'm working from home, but still. People can't see me like this.

And something changes in Said's tone. Is it possible, I mean with the throwing up . . .

I've got to go.

Wait. Is there any chance . . . ?

I feel like throwing up now. She hangs up and returns to her email.

Two days later a bubble-wrap envelope comes in the mail. Victoria doesn't seem to recognize the handwriting. She tears it open to find a small box wrapped in lined paper. Inside is a pregnancy test kit and a note: *Just try this. It's nothing just to try it. You need to know. I hope I haven't overstepped anything in doing this. S—.* She puts it on the kitchen table, where it sits for a few more days.

The next time Victoria opens her laptop I look for the date on the row of icons at the bottom of the screen. August 20. I've been her shadow for two months. It is hard to keep track of time when I have no responsibilities. Time seems both free and wasted. It becomes overly comfortable, but that comfort has now started surrendering to dread, especially because of Said's suggestion.

I know nothing about pregnancy and I know nothing about babies and children. Etti and I must have discussed it at times, but I don't recall details from any conversations we had. My impression is that Etti didn't want to have children, or even a single child, though she never stated it outright. What female artist could carry on her practice while raising a child, and who could recover a career after leaving it for several years? I can't think of any of Etti's artist friends who have had kids. It's as though they have to submit all of their experience into building their art careers. There is no way they could offer that attention to another person.

Perhaps it is simply that Etti didn't want children of her own. She worked with high-school students, she loved working with them, I think she actually grew to love them. But in her projects she is able to determine exactly how much time they spend together. She has her time of influence on a younger generation, and maybe that is enough.

As though it were now the object standing between herself and the future, Victoria finally removes the slender white device from the box and smooths out the folded instructions against the table, glancing back and forth between them and the device before stuffing them back in the box. She takes the device and its packaging to the bathroom, sits on the toilet and places it between her legs. I don't really see what she does, but she botches it somehow. She rinses off her hand and looks in the mirror. Her face is utterly ruined.

I'm surprised when she tries again, a few minutes later. She holds the device up to the light. What happens is subtle, but something does happen, a change creeps into view. The area between the arrows, at first white, darkens to grey. She continues to hold the device in the air but nothing more happens. The area remains grey. If anything it lightens a little. She takes the instructions from the box and rereads them. If the result is positive, it reads, the area between the arrows turns blue; if negative, pink. The strip remains an indeterminate grey.

What happens next sets me off balance, makes me realize that I have no insight into her thoughts. She drops the device on the floor and gazes point-blank at the mirror. She leans forward to get her face within a foot of the glass, and shouts: You fucking dick! You fucking dick! You fucking fuck! Fucking fuck! You fucking dick! She is looking through herself to some other side of the mirror, and before her eyes glaze over in tears, we share this terrible moment that casts us both as performers and audience. Then, flattening her hand, she begins pounding her palm against the counter, smacking it over and over again, and putting her face down near it so that she can see the hand meet the counter, punishing some invisible thing between her hand and the laminate surface.

Classplaza

One evening at Classplaza, after the teens had gone home for the day, I was left thinking about Etti and her spaces, and the way she interacted with her youth. It struck me that she was utopian in her work. She wanted to come up with an ideal way of being together with other people, where everyone was active and could safely express opposing ideas. Her utopia was a process that never ended. It would have come out of the blue when I said, Did you know that you're utopian? She thought I was joking, maybe because she had been living with her ideas for so long and couldn't see what they looked like from the outside. Or maybe the work was so exhausting to her, she would never recognize its ideals.

Even though she brought me to these hopeless places, I found it hard not to love the utopian in her.

She was in one of the metal-framed office chairs reading a magazine article about her work, and I could see she was not happy.

After finishing the article she opened her computer and began writing – it could only have been a message to F.

The article was about one of Etti's pieces, called *The Goal Is To No Longer Be a Teen*. With a group of high school students, Etti had developed a methodology for being in a school situation without fully succumbing to its negative, unjust or contradictory structures.

The central claim of the author was that it is impossible for one generation to teach a younger generation, and that therefore the premise of her work, even in her minimal presence as an artist-pedagogue, was misplaced. The only way teenagers could learn in that situation, he claimed, would be in opposition to whatever she offered. Teens themselves are the ones needing to figure out a new paradigm by which to approach a situation. The author of the article coined the term 'the teen entelechy' to describe some kind of adolescent inner-force that aims at the overthrow of their parents' generation, rejecting the materiality and ideas that they have grown up with, along with all the hypocrisies that are so familiar to them. The teen entelechy is a force for societal change that fully embraces negative thinking. It embodies a rejection of what came before. But the entelechy cannot be guided by someone of an older generation, not even someone like Etti.

The term sounded so good that people would jump on it, I thought. It had a lightning bolt sound to it. It sounded so good, but in fact was totally empty. It would be used and then people would tire of it, and it would disappear. I considered saying it out loud to let her know I shared in her frustration. And I hesitated, thinking that maybe the article would benefit her work. Even though the author had used the term to take down her entire practice, it would draw attention to it, perhaps giving it extra life.

I put the magazine down and said, The teen entelechy.

She looked over, and her expression was not one of recognition of my solidarity. It was something else, not of comfort, but of annoyance. If a look could speak words, it surely said something like this: There was a time, in fact most of our time together, that I would listen to you and take what you said seriously. You would engage me with your opinions, even when you expressed them incoherently, even when they were half-formed, even when they were speculative. We would talk with a kind of equality because we both had a lot going on. But now that we have been together for several years and now that I have witnessed your opinions for those years without them being paired with experience out in the world, I am no longer willing to listen. You haven't earned your right to an opinion. You haven't put yourself out there for so long. You are very far from that utopia that you imagine me in.

That's what I believed I saw in her eyes. I would write these lines of her thoughts, which came so easily to me despite how little we actually said to each other. I don't know what she really thought as she glared at me from across the interior of Classplaza.

Etti

Are you finding everything to be comfortable here on board the *Nancy*? Caslon asks.

I suppose so. Sure. I mean I haven't really thought about it. Everything is fine.

But are you happy here?

Yes. Happy enough. All of a sudden this seems like a very personal question. It seems more about me at a time when I imagined we'd be talking about you. I'm here for you.

Yes, of course. But it's important for me to know. I want everyone on board the *Nancy*, all of the people I've hired, to be happy.

Well, I'm not unhappy.

There's a military term, Caslon says. *Esprit de corps.* The state of being part of a greater whole, being a small part of a greater body whose power comes from the parts orienting into positive psychic alignment. I don't really know the minimum number of people needed to be considered a greater, discrete body. Definitely more than one. Let's say for the sake of this that the minimum number is two, though it's probably more since the problem with two is that it immediately sets up oppositions, or contradictions, or antinomies. So let's say more than two. The individual must let go of misgivings that he or she has in order to perform well as part of the whole. In other words the needs of the whole can only be satisfied if each of the parts is working well with each of the other parts. Signs of unhappiness in one part can affect all parts. Unhappiness can be disastrous because of its incredible tendency to spread.

But of course this is not a military operation, he continues. I don't mean to say that we have to give up our individuality in order for life onboard the *Nancy* to work. But it's something that's been on my mind recently.

Right, Etti says. I understand.

Caslon looks at her, inviting her to say more. But Etti doesn't say more.

I want to hear what you have to say.

Well, I'm used to something very different from what you're

saying. I mean that in situations in which I work, in my work as an artist, happiness doesn't often come into the equation. But then the people I collaborate with are not my employees. Are you happy?

It is a difficult question. There was a time when I was not happy, so I tried to do something about it. And then my solution caused me to be even more distraught. Maybe I've been using the wrong word in 'happiness.' Maybe what I mean is something like 'useful' or 'satisfied.' Satisfaction, as in having no desire for things to change from how they are.

When they arrive at the games room, Caslon turns the lights on, up high. The room feels incredibly impersonal for all of its games tables and apparatuses.

Etti, I must confess some things to you. Let's go sit over there. And they pass the billiard tables and sit across from each other on the long flat settees.

I become bored very easily. A few months ago, maybe more than a few months ago now, I had a crisis over my boredom. I could not experience enough life, nothing would satisfy me. You see, I have a kind of mania for the present that cannot be satisfied by material goods and extravagant living. I need to penetrate deeply into things. There is a kind of first-hand experience that I live for but that has to keep changing. I hit a point at which I could think of no way to be satisfied.

So I came up with this idea. There would be two of me. And through the two of us we would experience the world doubly. *I* would experience the world doubly. One of me could hang out on the yacht with all of the things that give me immediate pleasure, and the other could hang out in cities, among strangers, poor people, the people who are tossed out of society – the way Sherlock Holmes would go among paupers in opium dens, and pass out against walls among them. And then he could hang out at parties of the super-wealthy like myself, and then with artists and writers struggling for attention. At least that is how I imagined us starting.

The idea came from one of my friends. We were having a drink on the deck of his yacht, when all of a sudden a guy comes up who looks like him, dressed impeccably, the same way as my friend. Had I seen him in the street, I would have thought this guy looks a lot like my friend. In fact he looks too much like my friend to be his brother, because familial likeness is a strange phenomenon. Or he looks just like my friend at a glance but once in motion nothing seems right, the muscles don't carry through in the right way. He doesn't engender my friend, no matter how similar he looks.

Then, throwing me off further, another guy comes across the deck, also dressed the same and with the same haircut, et cetera, and he joins us too. To this point my friend has kept a poker face, but now he lets go and howls with glee. He says, For my safety. Sometimes I need two of them.

And then he just sits there smiling, letting me take it all in. There was something ridiculous about seeing the three of them together, because the two doubles looked like cheap or kitschy portraits of my friend. When they were all lined up like this, there was a sense in which they didn't really even look like each other. I mean, these guys were highly trained, they were doing the right things, but what I saw in my friend's face was central, and what I saw in theirs was peripheral. They were aliens compared to him. They all had a laugh, and the laughs were not very similar. Yet if you asked someone about the three of them, they might say yes, they look identical, because that would seem to be the correct answer.

It was all kind of grotesque, and we continued drinking, the four of us, and the longer I examined the others the more it confirmed my belief that their differences were not just in the visible, and in how they spoke, and in their manner and so forth, but in their expression of humanity. Maybe it was because of the contrast between the way they were meant to look and their all-too-visible failings as human beings, as doubles for a supremely rich guy. I did not envy my friend in having these guys around.

That night I stayed on his yacht. The *Ava*, he calls it. *Avenir*. I went to bed and my mind was racing from the alcohol. I wished that I had gone to bed earlier, had not stayed up with these guys, but I didn't want to be rude to my friend. He is very powerful and we met not all that long ago, and I suppose I didn't have full trust in him. These feelings must have compelled me to stay – I wanted him to think I trusted him, despite the many versions of himself that he presented that night. Things are so often complicated with new friends.

This is when the idea hit me about a second self. I wanted the opposite of what my friend had. A body double was perverse.

I wanted to experience a second self that could be elsewhere when I was in a situation like that on the *Ava*. I wanted to be in two places at once. I wanted a double presence.

Caslon pauses for effect, or so that Etti can absorb what he has just said, and Etti is looking at him as neutrally as she can, though thinking that perhaps a single presence is already so much. She says to Caslon, Go on.

I did some research. I did everything myself to avoid anyone else knowing about the idea. It was all top secret and still is, except that you need to know about it. I went to an island in the South China Sea. DNA was taken from my body and developed in a laboratory. A man was made. My memory was transferred to this second self. I didn't want to know all the details of the making of him. I have no idea how it was accomplished but these scientists pulled it off as though it were routine. My second self was completed without any major hurdles.

Though he came to me fully formed, he did come to me naked, with no belongings, no money, no source of income. I wanted him to be independent, in a sense. He needed to be able to go off on his own to experience life simultaneously with me. So I had a bank card made for him, a second credit card, and he withdrew as necessary, just as I would. This seemed like the obvious thing to do. I didn't give it a second thought. And I sent him off.

But I immediately knew that things were not as I'd planned. I'd expected to have more direct access to his experience than what unfolded in reality. I'd expected that I would experience the world doubly. What I actually have, however, is a second person who is very like me but whose perspective I don't experience the world through. In other words, I have to ask him about what he has done in the same way that you would have to ask a friend. This was an awful blind spot in my plan. A total failure in my thinking. To me it seemed like an obvious outcome to what the scientists had accomplished.

Well. At first it was not awful. I was disappointed that I wasn't immediately experiencing the second life, but I thought that a connection would grow so that I would begin seeing through his eyes and so forth. And I enjoyed hearing about his excursions, his partying and so on, and I enjoyed telling him about mine. But things changed. I started to get impatient, to hate the process, especially because there was no sign of our minds growing into one. And he, I assume, was feeling the same way. For a while we drifted from each other, circulating in groups of my friends that didn't know each other, different scenes altogether. But when we did see each other, we would look upon each other with disgust. We became antagonistic, not wanting to know anything about what the other had done. At times I would hear about him from other people – from our common friends who believed he was me. I'd hear that he'd given an opinion on something that was similar to my own yet marginally different. That's not really what I would say, I would think. That's not my true opinion. Even this slight difference irritated me, and I began to resent him.

Still, my reputation flourished from this doubling. In a sense I *was* experiencing double, but not from my perspective: from everyone else's perspective. I was doing twice as many things.

I was at twice as many parties, at twice as many art openings. Sometimes I would appear in magazine scenester shots at two different parties from the same night. Twice as many football matches. Twice as many restaurants. I was out there. It's funny, but a mere doubling of oneself really makes people notice. Imagine there being two of you, what you could do with that.

But it was not his wandering, his partying and so forth that bothered me most. Those things irked me a little but I could still celebrate his life as an extension of mine. It was when he started to slow down that I got worried. Something must have happened to cause the slow down, but it was surprisingly hard to investigate because people weren't aware that there were two of me, and I didn't want to go around asking people if I myself had been behaving strangely. He had done something, or someone had done something to him, but I had no idea what. And then one day his life just ground to a halt. He returned to the *Nancy* and insisted on staying on board, watching television. He watched art house cinema and sports, and then Hollywood movies and porn and sports. He would constantly be in the games room watching TV, sometimes playing foosball or table tennis with the crew, doing drugs, asking about how to get prostitutes on board. Things a teenager or twenty-year-old would do.

When it formed a pattern, when his life effectively became static, I had to confront him. I wasn't sure how to approach him though, as he was not like my employees. He was kind of like an employee, but he was also me, and I am the boss.

What was I to do? I couldn't stay with him. I couldn't babysit him. So one day I found him here in the games room and asked him to follow me to my office. This was surely one of the most embarrassing moments of my life. I talked to him like a concerned friend. I tried to negotiate with him. I said, You need to get back out in the world and experience life. This was the softest most fostering way of saying it, and I had no idea how he would react, as I myself would react very badly to this suggestion. He made some excuses about needing a break. This was just a hiatus, he insisted. Nothing more. I didn't know what to do next, so I suggested we meet every morning to touch base. Just a coffee together. Just a chat about how we were feeling. He agreed to this and left my office.

At this point in Caslon's confession it occurs to Etti to ask: Did you want me to be recording this?

No, definitely not. This is for you to know, but I don't think it should be down on paper. At least not right now. We need to talk about other things first. Consider this as a clearance of shit that has piled up.

It turned out that we didn't have that much to talk about in our daily meetings over coffee, Caslon continues. He still wasted his days in the games room. He managed to get prostitutes on board, fast food flown in by helicopter. I would stare at that all too familiar face while extracting these mundane facts of his life. I finally said fuck it to struggling with him. I said, Let's do this. Let's read the newspaper together. So I brought in two copies of the same paper and suggested we choose articles to discuss. It seemed like a simple thing. I thought it would be a good starting point. Moreover, I was curious to see exactly how different our opinions were, how far his had strayed from my own.

So we would read about an intervention by Femen, the feminists who go around topless and painted up. We would read about the decline of the Eurozone. We would read about new planets and gravitational waves and whatever else physicists were uncovering. We would read opinion pieces from the Left and the Right, about race and climate change and so on.

I had to face the fact that some of his opinions and behaviours were my own, even when I did not like them or did not want to admit to them. I had to guess when he was withholding his true opinion in the way that I might, or when he was lying in the way that I would. But it was clear, in spite of all these possibilities, that his thoughts had already deviated from my own, and with astonishing speed.

It made me ask myself: when had I developed my opinions toward the world? At what stage in my life? But, more importantly, I thought, what year did my opinions start to solidify? What year in history? I honestly had no idea, Etti. But it was a question that began keeping me up at night.

Most important for me now was this: even though he had my memories built into him, I feared that his birth into the present must have sent him flying off into some other direction, in terms of his opinions and actions. Was it possible that his formative years were the present, while mine were twenty or thirty years ago? Was he of a completely different generation from me?

Something really came to a head one day when we were reading an article about a new yacht under construction. I had heard rumours of this yacht, and the rumours were wild, but the details were being kept super secret. This yacht was apparently very intelligent. They were calling it a yacht of 'multiple intelligences.' It could read all kinds of things about the people on board. The engineer had taken all the current research on biometrics and made the yacht the most sensitive object on the planet, attuned to almost imperceptible facial movements, body language, personal humidity, skin microbiota, the vicissitudes of human emotion and reactions. Not only could it essentially read the active thoughts of its passengers, it could also delve into their subconscious, their ideologies. The article did not say what the purpose of this would be, so we speculated about why such a smart vessel would be desirable.

And he said: For the thrill of it. For the thrill of being outed among your peers. That's an amazing idea. Kick back and be read through and through. It would be like an orgy. Invite all your friends. Get a load of people together. Then let the yacht read everyone. All personality, all volition, all memory, is laid bare and allowed to get it on in a mass of personal promiscuity. Total soul exposure.

He seemed one step ahead of me, and I thought about what he said, and all my desire for new experience, and I wondered if I could go to that place he was talking about. To that orgy. At first I was carried away by his unbridled enthusiasm. I thought, yes. Fucking yes! But then I thought, there is no way I could do that. And I wondered if he were just exaggerating, or whether he would really go there. So I pressed him, and when he said 'absolutely,' I could see that he was dead serious. He said: I want to know everything about those people without having to talk to them.

I suggested that we break for the day, and that we hold off on future meetings. I needed to do something on shore, I told him.

I cancelled his credit card. I set him up as an employee, paying him every two weeks in the same way that I pay everyone else on the yacht. A direct payment into a new bank account that was his alone. He was pissed off at me and I told him to embrace it. I can't tell you how good this felt. I was relieved. But more than relieved, I felt bolstered. I did not realize it at first, but I came to understand that I enjoyed wielding power over him more than anyone else on my crew. Perhaps it is because he is closer to being my equal than anyone else. I'm still not sure.

Needless to say I expect that you will not repeat this to anyone, Caslon says.

Of course, Etti says. Etti might have been wondering if this were a test, or whether she just happened to provide an ear for his story. She doesn't know what to do with what she has heard, whether to be shocked by the route that Caslon took to fulfill his desires, whether to accept it as the full truth, and whether she should be burdened by the world he has thrown upon her.

Moreover she feels for the double, the unfair world he has been dropped into. How can she do this memoir thing knowing of this imbalance? And yet. There is no going back now, she thinks. Caslon has made this so.

That is how they began the morning two days after Etti witnessed their skirmish. Caslon had entered the dining hall at breakfast, as she was finishing her fruit and yoghurt, sipping coffee, and she saw him as he entered. He came to her and sat down, much as he had done when they met a few days back on Suomenlinna, and as on Suomenlinna he looked a touch dishevelled, though this time it showed in his eyes rather than his hair and clothing. His face distracted Etti, what seemed like a matte area by his cheekbone, as if the area was airbrushed with very subtle makeup. She tried to determine which Caslon she was facing, at first connecting the possible makeup to the face that was hit by the cellphone, then wondering if other blows were exchanged after she had left, and still moments later speculating that if there was just the one blow, whether the Caslon who was left untouched had put on cover-up the same as the other, so that they both wore the same irregularity. But, she thought, this was the original one, so far as the original one was the one she first met on Suomenlinna.

He would like to begin in a few minutes, he said, she could bring her coffee with her, that's all she would need. Nelson would lead her to his office. Her heart rate increased, feeling all of a sudden relieved but unprepared, and perhaps this combination made her excited. It set the right tone for her.

The morning after witnessing the Caslons fight – the day before Caslon's confession – she asked around about where the yacht was heading. The staff of the *Nancy* would not say anything. They were indifferent in their responses. They didn't know. When she asked if they didn't know or simply wouldn't say, she was told they were not at liberty to say anything. She asked who she should talk to about it. Like one of the crew? she offered. Like the captain or something? I don't know, was the answer.

That afternoon she ran into the same woman she'd sat beside on the night of the party, right before seeing Caslon. She was almost unrecognizable now in her bikini top and linen skirt. Excuse me, Etti said, and before she could say more, the woman asked, I think that Caslon hire you to learn English to me?

He didn't mention that, Etti said.

I think that it chances that Caslon is not every time clear intentionally.

What did he say to you?

Something in his look suggest I need tutoring.

Do you want to improve your English?

It is okay. But why not?

Perhaps he could hire you an English tutor.

Perhaps, but I don't think it is in me. Maybe it be good to me though. It seems like correct move. I just keep expecting something come my way, something Caslon send. This time I think it you.

The woman had what almost anyone would recognize as an amazing body. Her face was long, and maybe a little masculine. Her skin was white, so white compared to Etti's, and despite wearing the bathing suit, she was not well tanned. She wore mirrored sunglasses that distracted Etti as they talked. Have you been on the yacht for long? Etti asked.

For a while.

You must know something about the yacht then.

Some things.

Do you know what direction we're going?

I don't know. I see that we are going east because the sun is coming up over where we are going. Caslon point this out to me. But I do not know where. I think maybe no other way from Bay of Finland unless to Russia. We are going slow. Really slow.

I see, Etti said. Do you know who I could ask about it – where we're headed?

I think maybe Caslon keep it to self. She smiled and Etti had no idea why her smile was so powerful and seemed so directed toward her.

You want to come to my quarters? the woman said.

Etti followed her down the main stairs and through a door

she hadn't taken before, and Nelson followed. She noticed another man alongside Nelson, whom she assumed to be the woman's Nelson. They entered the woman's room, leaving their attendants outside.

It was much larger than Etti's room and far more lived in, with clothing thrown about and some photos on the wall, but it was all designed in the same style – whatever style that was, swank and smoothed over, super-precise – that she had become accustomed to on the yacht.

Now that the woman removed her sunglasses, their eyes were allowed unmediated contact. The woman's gaze was solid.

I would offer something but it not custom here for one guest to offer another guest something. They sat on comfortable plastic chairs.

Did you want to show me something? Etti asked.

No. Just talking. You are writer? Or film person like Caslon suggest at the party night?

No. An artist. I work with teens.

Artist teacher?

Sort of, Etti said. What do you do?

Well now, hard to say. I came on the yacht, and now it feel far from knowing.

How did you end up here?

Caslon picked me up in maybe four months in past. Not really pick me up more his friend take me by motored boat here. I was with his friend and his friend visit Caslon. Still I am here.

What else?

Perhaps it long-wise story. But I tell some of it. You mean in long view?

Sure, long view. Whatever you like.

Long view then. It like a history. In long view I feel I need explain thinking more. I have thought much about this question. What bring me here has real lead-up. It was not economic crush of 2008 that made all this happen against me. But it was not occupation movements that happened across the world either. And not either the coming of the words 1% and 99% in togetherness that made the big change to me like revelations. Because I hear words 1% and 99% long before change happen against me. What it was was an arising in consciousness of idea of economy and economy difference by so many people who maybe were denying such root of effects in past. In other word, it was not event but widely spreading simple idea and idea reached rich people. If I read right that is what made change for me.

The story begin with a man, one person who in past was like others who did not recognize inequations. He saw me in the street when I was getting food from outside of grocery store at nighttime. He in the black car, driving around market neighbourhood. He ask me if I look for food in the trash. I say it is fine, but he sees I have the plastic bag full in heavy fruit. He ask if I would want a real meal. I think about the bag of bruised soft fruit and am tired and say that yes a real meal. For certain I look hard at him. I see his face in rolled window. I feel like things bad in my life though I think back and say no they not change in time before and after economic crush. Again he ask about real meal. So I just do it at risk of my life because my life at moment feels not like a life even though a smile on my face.

This is Caslon you are talking about?

No. Not Caslon. Not him. Other man. This other man who pick me up is expat and not speak well in my language all so much. He identify in age with Generation X for certain. He was Gen-Xer, I see it because I see them in American television during evenings, kind of ruling world now. On other hand I tell you this story because I want to say again the main point. This guy has feeling to capture me because of the air in the time. He said that he is making change in his life and he has longer view now because of air in time. Before he think that history in air is gone, but later he feel like it in air again. And he want to seize air in time. He look in me something he needs to experience help in. And so he take me to his big apartment at top of high-rise. That where he live. At least events that where he live some of times though it turn out not most of times. He give me extra room and key and clothing already there in apartment room on rack.

I had not think of air in time before he brought it in that night. I look at his apartment with its big windows viewing city and I eat the meal he buy on way there. We sit at the kitchen island. He talk to me about air in time while I eat and look about open room. Before I think of one day and another day and then another day. I never hear of the 1 and the 99 before. And then I hear and still I don't relate to 1 or even 99 and never think of air in time. I think I outside of 1 and 99 though adding to 100 leaves no outside. That takes me some times to get. Some times 1 and 99 do not add to 100, or some times total exceeds 100 even in percent scenario. If some make most money and others work and make little money there is also some person who not works and not make money but also not feed the 1%. Some people are impossible and I come to think I myself to be impossible.

But he take numbers personally, as though he encounter something big and it change him. The eye-look of encounter with big one. I wonder, what is there for him before 1 and 99?

And then I start feeling there is more to it. I become worried that for him I need to be 99, that if he discover I am not part of it all, he will abandon me, that my value for him be the part of equation opposite him. That he going to kick me out and I will return to previous life. And yet I also begin worry that him taking me in is like conversion of me from outside 99 to inside 99, so that if I am not 99 at first, I am now because now he gives me a kind of salary in exchange for me being in his apartment. But I don't know. Still the possible chance that he discover I am not part of it before will make him feel foolish and throw off his moment of great lightening. And with that I am in a big trouble. But he seem not to clue in.

I then live there in that apartment for while. There is food in fridge and money in envelopes. I watch TV during day and night. I am now domestic animal cut off from previous life, lying around high above city and everyone. I am on internet and watch explaining people on YouTube. I try and understand more. I go out onto street and look at front pages of news. It is a new life for me like I never imagine before. I never dream man like him carry me away. That he not want anything from me. That he want me as I am but at same time makes me something else. Something else that sees farther away things.

You said that the guy was Caslon's friend and that he took you here?

Oh, here. Let me say first thing is, here on yacht I really not think of air in time. Not even of one day and another day. I don't know where it all goes now. It like there is no air in time and no day after day. I don't know what it like. Of course there is TV and on TV is news that gives a feel of air in time. But in man's apartment I really feel time in air, I above so many others in physical way, up in sky. From balcony I see small people in daily life. I see poor far neighbourhood. But here, no.

What happened to the guy?

Oh he left on boat the next day. There is nothing there to worry about. I think he a good guy but he see something in me and then see something different in me. Well no. Something happens that is seeable. The guy comes by one day to apartment. I am out. When I return he sees me in new lighting, he says.

I don't know why he brings me to Caslon and leaves. He think maybe Caslon interested in me, but Caslon not quite interested in me. Maybe he sort of interested in me. He says I'm perfect, then something change in him, maybe he has lightening in him, and he looks at me differently. He stroke my arm and look uncertain. I don't know what he thinks. He not the same each time I see him. I think maybe he irritated by my English, and then he hire you. But you are not a tutor for me. I don't know what I am doing here now.

What do you want to do?

Like I say, it feel like nothing in air here. But I have taste for this nothing in air. If before I was fully buried in waste and hungry, now there is no heavy covering at all, and I am eating and all. But there is nothing here but the party and the games room. I know I need to leave, but I feel I am forgotten to Caslon and to the bigger world. Maybe we become friends you and me and I ask you what you think I must do.

Her face, Etti continued to observe, was strangely unblemished given her time on the streets. Pale and smooth.

Why don't you ask the questions you want to ask? F said to Etti. And Etti thought, I don't want to shut things down. I almost asked the woman for her name, but even something as simple as her name might shut some things down, close some things off. I want to keep this woman undefined for as long as possible.

And I myself need to remain vulnerable. I need to answer to the woman truthfully should she ask me anything. The truth was the greatest tool in disarming whomever she was talking to. The truth split space open enough to change the direction of a conversation, of a negotiation, of a relationship. If the standard way to be with a stranger was to be cagey, to avoid the possibility of closeness, she had to be the opposite. Unless she was the opposite of the norm, she thought, all she would produce would be the norm. And the norm was hazardous to all.

I feel something starts to fail in my situation, the woman now said. Caslon, last time I see him say maybe there is something for me to do. He say wait, and he will get back to me. But this is weeks past. Do I wait for a maybe? Can you give a good sight to me?

I'm not sure, Etti says. He didn't give you any idea what he has in mind?

Maybe he train me for something.

What if you left?

What then, what when I on land in some other place? Part of my feeling says stay until there is sign saying leave. But there is just yacht every day. I feel like a part of yacht, like it swallow me in sameness of itself.

I wish I could help out but I don't know what to say, Etti said.

How about English?

Yes, Etti said, maybe I can help with English. We can talk if you like. It felt like a natural time for Etti to leave, so she got up and said goodbye to the woman. On the way out the woman said to Etti, Please, come tomorrow.

But the next day Caslon grabbed her from the dining hall before it could happen.

Etti and Caslon move from the games room to a bright office-like space, where they sit in light chairs.

Caslon asks, Where does a starting place come from?

He seems to be asking himself the question. But Etti considers the question, and says, From a lot of places.

That's true. A starting place is an exciting thing, right?

Yes.

Because a starting place is an opening that is all potential. One place it often comes from is a question or a problem. Without a question or a problem we just go on as is, without looking for a starting place. The world without questions just carries on by sheer inertia.

Etti nods.

You asked me a question, Caslon goes on. You asked, Would you like me to ghostwrite your memoir? That is what you asked in that first email that you sent. And I said yes, and that in a way is our starting place. I said yes because I liked the idea. But if I think about it now, it's clear that the problem the starting point emerges from is not my need to record my life – though your question about writing a memoir does raise that possibility – but your need for money. The problem is that you need money, and the answer is to write my memoir.

Etti is smiling about this because she, for her part, likes when someone reveals her base intentions. She enjoys being outed.

I don't mean anything by it. But I was thinking, before we met, that we need to reorient our starting point so that the answer to 'I need money' is not 'Caslon's memoir.' We could use a different problem altogether, but then the answer will likely not be, 'Let's write Caslon's memoir.' Perhaps we need to skip those starting places and move forward. How about this very obvious question: What are you doing here on board the *Nancy* with me, Caslon Maxim?

I could say, Etti says, Talking about writing Caslon's memoir.

Somehow in that we come full circle. Let's begin with the question 'Why write Caslon's memoir?'

How about this, Etti says, Let's answer it through the act of actually writing the memoir. Caslon seems delighted by the answer, and Etti gets a little charge from this, though wonders if now Caslon has talked his way out of paying her. You still mean to pay me, she says.

Money is whatever, he says. I'm concerned about how we're actually going to do this.

Caslon watches her in silence. He has brought her to his office, which is a long narrow room, entirely white, with no curves, and bookshelves running one side of it, books stacked in columns by colour. The source of light in the room is unclear at first, but when the eyes adjust they find that it is emanating from the walls themselves, and the ceiling and the floor, so that there is a soft unified glow everywhere. There is no desk, just the two simple plastic chairs that Etti and Caslon sit in. Caslon pulls a laptop from a slim bag and passes it to Etti, who leaves it closed on her lap.

For me the real problem, above all other problems in you raising the memoir question, is what form will it take? You may have gathered I have a thing for the present, a kind of obsession. I read a lot, and I have noticed that writers are also obsessed with the present. They use the present tense in their writing. Perhaps the present tense feels more real to everyone. That may be true. Or perhaps it's not about realism but intensity. Only the present feels intense. But the present tense no longer feels all that intense. No longer is it closer to the real. It feels like the dull realization of the constant present.

And so one of my stumbling blocks, Caslon continues, is what tense to write the memoir in. This is where you can help me. I wish there were a tense that is more present than the present tense, one step ahead of the present tense, but only a fraction of a second ahead of it, a squint past it – connected enough to the present to be recognizable, yet with a jolt of immediacy. A tense at the limit of the reader's recognition, but that propels them into another world.

I've thought about the future tense, he says. But we're used to the future tense, and we recognize the dishonesty in it. As one writer wrote, it is the tense of speculation but not of the truth.

Is it possible, I have been asking myself, to invent a tense just slightly ahead of the present tense? Caslon looks to Etti for her response, and for the first time she feels Caslon asking something of her that is well beyond her capabilities.

What might that look like? she asks.

I kept thinking about it, he says, and realized no. For one thing, you can't invent a tense – no one would recognize it. It would be gibberish and have the exact opposite effect of what I desire, because it would be impenetrable to any reader. It would be opaque. What I want is a language that is most transparent, like a clear northern sky, yet charged with the energy of the just about to happen.

I've seen some films recently in which there was almost no dialogue. Just actions without explanations. One thing to the next and the viewer doesn't know why anything is happening or how one event is connected to the next, yet it all feels very very real. No interiority for the characters. Those films feel closer to the tense that I want to find than anything I've seen in writing. It was as if the director knew that by adding language the films could never feel as present, as about to happen, as they did with almost no talking at all. In moments when talk actually happened in the films all their magic was lost. The life of them fell earthbound. So I wonder, perhaps we should develop the language of this memoir *without* language at all. Maybe you have some ideas about that. What do you think, Etti?

Etti is silent. She is likely intrigued, wondering if there is any direction that they could take that would satisfy these desires of his. She thinks that there is no way to record a life without language, but at the same time she will do anything she can to find an answer.

I think we should begin very simply, she says. Concretely, in the present. She already knows that Caslon has no interest at all in going into his past, in telling the story of his life, and that her proposal to write his memoir was simply a starting point for him thinking about his life in the present, by way of which he would aim for something in opposition to her suggestion. And this all made total sense to her now, seeing this man at the brink of middle age, still young, still restless, not at all ready to go back into his past. When she had written her introductory email to him, she realizes now, she had pictured a much older man, not someone of her own generation. In the wake of their conversation, the whole idea of memoirs seems so antiquated. The word raised the image of aging rock stars and former politicians. Surely no one from my generation will want to write a memoir, she thinks. No one truly of my generation.

The one thing I am certain about, Caslon says, is that I don't want my life resolved in a story, one that will set the falsehood of such resolutions in stone. A key will be that it's undigested. I will not endeavour to make meaning out of my life. Somehow it must be unfiltered. But on the other hand I believe it needs some limits, like a start and an end. And it can't just be a live webcast of my life. I mean, hasn't every version of what I want been done and been exhausted within a short few years of technology making it possible? We have to have faith that this is not the case. Perhaps there needs to be a sense in which we don't really know what we are doing. Maybe that would be the 'just about to happen' of the memoir.

And now he seems elsewhere, remains distant for some time. Etti sits with the closed computer on her lap, soaking in the sci-fi radiance of the room.

I saw, Etti, at the party a few nights ago, he says, that you didn't agree with me about Zidane and our generation. The look on your face told me that you disagreed. I want to know more about that. Perhaps that should be our starting place.

Okay, she says. All that look meant was that I didn't relate to Zidane the way you did, so I don't think I was part of the generation that it brought together.

Can you think of a moment like Zidane's, for you and your generation?

I can't, she says. That night of the party, after you left, I kept thinking about it. Well into the night until it made me delirious.

Maybe it's good, he says. Maybe it's better that we don't share the same generational moment. Maybe it adds to making you optimal for doing this memoir.

Let's say it does, Etti says.

I think that there is one step that we must take to begin with, and that is to disembark, to leave the *Nancy* for a little. Nothing is likely to happen on board the yacht. I mean, for sure nothing will happen on the yacht. That is the whole point of the yacht.

I need time to think, he says. But we will begin very very soon. Maybe we will begin, as you suggest, even before we know what we're doing. Caslon stands and heads for the door. We will begin on land. I'll let you know.

Victoria

Where that grey smudge fits among all the other things that surround me, I don't know. I understand it is a mark, a point, something that I must understand my life in relation to, but beyond that . . .

Beyond that it acts as a flag planted on a particular day, forcing me to look backwards, to the stretch of time before the bathroom. It affords a view of the young Victoria, of another world so far removed from Classplaza and the series of ad hoc residences Etti and I have lived in. It shows me that I have a past with Victoria. And even though it is so recent, I can't help but feel nostalgic for the last two months, as though they formed a honeymoon period. She has been my version of going away into some otherness, a mind clearance paired with new experience – perhaps Jan Melbrooks had this part right, or perhaps I see it this way because of him – just as our mothers and fathers read Castaneda and drove to the desert with an indigenous guide and hallucinogens, or read Hesse on their flight to India or Nepal, then trekked among the locals, accepting their generosity as a response to their own desire for spiritual insight, a pre-modern way of life. Has Victoria become my unknowing India? I wonder. In the same way that travellers abroad need to open up in order to experience the new world to its fullest, have I too opened up to her alien offerings? Have I climbed her sacred mountains wide-eyed and stepped barefoot into her sacred rivers and smiled at her people, whatever all that means?

I can't help but wonder, from my perspective abroad in the foreign land of Victoria, what my world will look like in the future. When my time with Victoria has ended, when I have reunited with Etti and we have moved into the city again, into a decent apartment, Etti having given up on her attempts to revitalize non-spaces, when, even, I have crossed paths with Josephine and we have stayed in touch for some time, becoming friends, exchanging stories about what it was like to be a shadow, how will I be more inside life? I can't help but look for that point on the horizon.

Maybe all of these imaginary travels are possible only because Victoria has completely disregarded me. I've been allowed to travel anonymously, experiencing the world without touching it without leaving a trace. But now that she's brought me into the picture, everything has changed. All of the fantasies fall away to the real horizon of Victoria and that point of grey. She has seen me.

The pregnancy test infuses Victoria with an awful energy, has her taping garbage bags over the mirrors, pouring scalding bath water over her skin. Has her inspecting her vagina with a hand mirror, staring at the area between her legs as though at any moment I will emerge as a grey-black swirl.

She sits at her computer for a long time before beginning a message to Said. *I have been hesitant to bring this up because it seems delicate, but I have a question about the job shadowing: could you tell me when it will end? Not that it's a problem. I mean, I am more than happy to be in this situation. I just –* and then she stops typing, and erases the message. She rephrases it, making it more direct, and erases it. Then another one: *Hi Eugenia, I'm writing with a question that I hope you can answer. It might be important to me but I'm not sure. Can you keep this to yourself? You were at the conference hall that day when the job shadows were assigned, weren't you? I think I saw you there at one point. If you were, do you remember the name of the guy who got up onstage and gave a speech? The life historian? I honestly can't remember his name but I want to find out about him. If you remember, please let me know. Thanks, Victoria. PS: Have you had any <u>effects</u> from your shadow?*

And then, before sending the message, Victoria erases her postscript. About 15 minutes later Eugenia responds: *Victoria, I couldn't remember the name of that guy so I asked around a little bit at the office for you. His name is apparently Yan Melbrooks or Yan Mel Brooks. Something like that. They got him in from the US. That's all I could find out. I would look him up online. Hope you're doing better soon.*

A minute or two later a third email arrives: *Hey Victoria, Eugenia was saying that you were wondering about the job shadowing fair? I had some questions myself, but some shit has gone down here in the past few days. Some shuffling among the uppers. It's hard to know who is in charge now. It seems like no one is in charge right now, or no one we know. People were let go. It was a major re-haul. Anyway, if I find out anything I'll let you know. Best, Taylor.*

Again she begins a message to Said. *I need your help. Please help me.* And this time she sends it.

She can barely get out of bed the next morning. She falls onto the floor, then proceeds in a half-walk, half-crawl, collapsing twice on the way to the washroom.

She finds it in herself to look up Jan Melbrooks on the internet. He has a website and a contact page, and she sends an email to him, and I guess she hopes that whoever reads the message will forward it to him. *I was a participant. I need help. I have a shadow. I'm sick from him. I think he's made me pregnant with some shadow monster. My job is at stake. My image. I need him gone. Please, please, respond to this message.*

I wait alongside her for the response. We wait and when it comes it is not from Melbrooks but from Learning Ecologies. An auto-reply message. *Said will be away from his desk for an indefinite period,* it reads.

Etti

She's been aware of the rain hitting the hood of her raincoat for ten or fifteen minutes, at the same time feeling her body rise and fall with the motorboat's front end. It must be a small motorboat again, and they are going very fast – whether that is just how small motorboats go or whether Caslon loves speed, she does not know. Perhaps he is going fast just because he can, because the velocity throws him deeper into the present, and even if that's not it, the heightened effect on the nerves is undeniable. What might otherwise have been time to herself, filled with reflections on what she might do with everything from the *Nancy*, the few things she collected and the task Caslon has given her, is occupied by the encroaching roar of the motorboat and a smattering of shouts carrying across the water from other boats or the shoreline.

The pitch of the motor drops and the boat slows, the motor

cuts out and they coast to what must be a stop. She takes off the blindfold as they have discussed in advance, pockets it and follows him along the wooden docks past small yachts and out through a locked gate. They are immediately met by a multi-lane avenue backed on the opposite side by undivided facades in pastels and greys. Caslon heads directly for a crosswalk where they wait by the heavy traffic, and once on the other side leads her through a grand archway, glancing back over his shoulder and allowing Etti also to glance back to see the massive river behind them, the new towers on its far bank supporting corporate signs that glow in Cyrillic.

Sometimes when she arrives in a foreign city she is aware of colour – here the people are mostly white – but whether she becomes self-conscious of her own ambiguous tone, her sort of olive-brown skin and dark hair, a variety that might have said Mediterranean to some and Middle Eastern to others, maybe South Asian to others, or a territory bordering Russia to others, or whether she feels so part of that something else called 'the art world' that she considers it only from a distance, is not clear. And though it has never overtly come up with Caslon she may wonder if it will come up, especially since Caslon seems to consider the details of a situation in a way that would not overlook her background, never mind her gender. If she was perfect for him, as he said she was, what made her so perfect? Perfection has made her uneasy. They arrive at a hotel where Caslon talks to a woman at the desk – he speaks to her in Russian before receiving a key card – and a hotel employee attends them on their elevator ride to the top floor, leaving them at the open door of the room. Not a huge room and somewhat baroque in stark contrast to the ultramodern otherworldliness of the yacht – whatever that difference means, Etti has no idea, yet likely sits with the dissimilarity as she considers where she will be expected to sleep. They leave their bags on the queen-sized bed and return to the street again, Caslon never looking at Etti, never talking to her, never giving any indication of her presence. There is a discipline in his silence toward her. He seems preoccupied but at the same time calm, as though he is at work.

Etti re-registers herself in relation to Caslon every few seconds, walking at his side, a bit back, three feet away, and this is all because, she thinks, she is unclear what her method is and so overcompensates in any way she can. Re-registering his mood, monitoring its subtle shifts – this while the strange city moves past them. She wonders if she can naturalize this concentration on a single other person so that it isn't a drain on her, so that she can freely drift in her own thoughts even as she attends her subject.

Caslon exits the commercial street, taking an entryway into a space that extends away from them as a dated but fancy mall atrium. At the architectural centre, by empty café tables and a glistening fountain, he pauses and surveys the shops. He crosses the space to a business whose front is fully walled-in by glass. Printed in vinyl along the back are the initials ОКАДБ. He enters and speaks to the woman at the counter. There is no one else around. The woman takes Caslon and Etti through to an office. A man behind a desk stands to greet Caslon, and Caslon responds in Russian and then English: I need to open an account for this woman here. I will be making deposits into her account on a weekly basis, and then moves into Russian again before saying, Please set it up to automatically deposit $5,000 American per week. And from that point on the men continue in the foreign language, occasionally exchanging what must be jokes, because they chuckle together. The man gets up and leaves for several minutes in which time Etti looks around the unnervingly empty office, still observing Caslon who waits in a relaxed pose, leaning and hanging one arm over the back of the chair. The man returns and carefully places a piece of paper on his desk, rotating it to face Etti. It says, 'ID,' and she pulls out her passport for him, and a few minutes later he hands it back in addition to a ОКАДБ bank card and a wireless keypad for activating the card. From then on he acts as if she is not there, exchanging a few more quick jokes with Caslon before Caslon gets up and they head out the door.

On the street again, she is jostled by other pedestrians. She replays their yacht conversation until hitting the point she wanted to review: that nothing happens on a yacht, and that is why they are on shore. In the moment she had believed that she'd understood everything, she tended not to let a conversation continue until she really understood what her interlocutor was saying, following its intent. Nothing could happen on a yacht, and that is what the yacht is for, he had said. The yacht is a world safe from everything going on outside of it, a place to drop out, to become an animal lying in the sun, drained of thought and volition. But nothing happening is a problem, he had said. They had come to this city because nothing like Zidane's head-butt could happen on the *Nancy*.

And though she doesn't know what the thing is that Caslon wants more than anything else to happen – because this, it had seemed to her, was the subtext of his statements – still she wishes she could say to him, having spent only this short period absorbing the city and feeling its instantaneous weight, feeling that every space into it is outside, that there is no inside, that this is absolutely the wrong place for the thing to happen, whatever that thing happens to be. She has never felt this way toward a city before, and it's unbelievable even to herself that she thinks this so soon after their arrival, never mind that she thinks it at all, but she has this dire reaction to being there. Though she hasn't seen a name of it anywhere she knows what city it is. And to her it does in fact feel like the yacht. A seemingly impossible belief to form, because a 300-year-old city where millions of people make their lives can in no way be like a state-of-the-art superyacht designed for a single ego. But in these first hours a carry-over feeling overwhelms her, a pressure in her gut, the taint of one thing echoed in the next. Maybe it is just Caslon's proximity. She wishes she could write it off as that – as the sameness he has brought with him. But already, so reactive is she to new places, it feels as though everything of this heavy city is already done, like there is no space for her, that the story is over, that it is all too much, that it is fucked up and that its fucked-up qualities speak so loudly that all of the potential for something to happen in it has passed.

They move off the main thoroughfare to another street whose five-storey buildings push on unbroken in their hybrid of crumbling opulence and zero-sum austerity. She wants to say, Let's go somewhere else. The matter of this city has already been overworked. But she can't say a word.

That first night, she and Caslon descend from street-level down cement steps into a series of cavernous rooms. A server attends to a few people at small tables. All of the cigarette smoke pools in the vaulted ceiling. In one corner Caslon finds a number of men who must be friends or associates, and as they sit he states something in Russian, and thereafter they pay no attention to her.

But it would be a fantasy to believe that they were not looking over at her now and then as they talked, as they nibbled at the hot dogs that were brought to the table, and thin slices of bread, and more frequently as the night progressed, or perhaps not more frequently but with gazes that protract and intensify. One face barely masks a near-violent urge to say something to her. But the man is never given the chance; even when Caslon goes to the washroom Etti follows. She is not away from him for a heartbeat.

As with nights to follow, Caslon later ends up at a club, hangs around with young women, drinks back pills in a private room, then gets up and leaves with a prostitute, and the three of them, Caslon, the prostitute and Etti, crowd in the back seat of a taxi on the way to the hotel. Leaning on the hotel room wall a few feet away, Etti observes Caslon and the woman doing their thing until the woman takes her exit and Caslon turns out the light, at which point she lies down in the cot at the foot of his bed. She never expected to see him with a prostitute, though it matches what he has described of his double, and then she thinks, but I should have known because surely what the double does he too would do. And she is surprised at herself for witnessing it all as objectively as she does, even when the woman glances over at her, making her moaning sounds, and their eyes meet, and something passes from the woman's eyes to hers – something that says, Etti might imagine, I know what I'm doing. What exactly is it that you are doing?

She is exhausted and cannot sleep. Her mind is on the bank, how doubt had been building in her when she'd entered with Caslon. But with the bank card in hand she felt a clearance of doubts, a soft release, the same release one experiences returning home from a foreign country. Her new reality is underscored, fully realized, with the introduction of a bank card and the wage that it signifies.

Five grand a week, F might be saying to her at this point. Five thousand dollars for following him around. Is this not the most rad job ever? F is half-serious and half-joking, because sometimes what is spoken is more a social offering than a guiding light, more about the act of edifying an interlocutor than presenting opposition.

She gets up from her cot and goes to one of the windows where light comes in from the night sky. On the ledge a few inches off the ground, just by her foot, there is a postcard. It's an old postcard with five panels on it. 'EEN VAKANTIE' in the centre of the five quaint, timeless images, and some tiny print on the back that looks like it might be Dutch or Danish. It seems like an ironic reprint that the hotel has made for its guests, but on closer look she sees it's authentically old, from the '60s. Its five somewhat random views are assembled as a portrait of what look to be healthy ways of living.

Before her flight to Finland, she left a note on the bed where Gil was guaranteed to see it. A job had come through, she wrote, something that would fill the gap. It was in Helsinki, a writing gig unrelated to her work, but which might transform into a new piece. She didn't know exactly where she'd be staying, but had her phone and computer with her. She would send a message. She didn't know how long she'd be, maybe a few months. And of course she didn't know how long he'd be either. He had disappeared often in the past, and she tolerated his disappearances, especially because he'd made them ever since she'd started seeing him. Even from an early date he'd taken off, leaving her at an opening and not contacting her for a couple weeks, and then when they started living together he would disappear for even longer periods. He would always return and they went on with their lives together.

It was not that she didn't feel something when he disappeared. She would miss him and perhaps worry about him, but then she would stand back a little and abstract him so that he became like a line on a map, a vector moving between points, an arc, a zigzag. But usually he was a steeply curved line, because he did always return. And at home he became a full person again, her life partner, she supposed, if anyone was one. At least a partner for a period before things changed. Before she could no longer register him.

And now she imagines that he has already returned to Class-

146

plaza, and that he experiences the abandonment that she every so often knew, and finding the letter on the bed he would likely first try to contact her, then worry about her and feel depressed about being in Classplaza alone, and leave Classplaza after a day of thinking about it.

From her place at the hotel window she hears Caslon shift his sleeping weight and looks around at him. Why would it matter, she thinks, if Caslon were to wake while she was at the window looking at a postcard? And yet she remains still and continues to observe him until he seems resettled, because it *would* matter, as unclear as their relationship may be. Perhaps it is clearer than she is conscious of.

Enough light enters the room to see a pen if there were one, at least to see one on a flat surface that the light from outside hits, the chest of drawers, the coffee table, the bedside tables, the credenza, but there is not one. Instead, an ashtray, a remote control for the TV, an old phone, another ashtray, two upside down glasses wrapped in plastic, a radio that looks like it's from the Soviet era. She slips the postcard under the elastic of her pyjama bottoms and returns to her barely existent bed.

This thing she now tries to summon has something to do with representation. The word has never come up with Caslon, but that is what he intends. I'm tasked with representing him, she thinks to herself. Even though not a conventional memoir, her work is representation. And even though there is no tangible material to apply, no paint or film, no signifying structure to deploy, she still needs to represent him. What comes to mind from her readings – what might be her ideal score – seems both simple and impossible: that the representation of the thing needs to be contiguous with the thing itself. The representer cannot lose sight of the original object. Otherwise, she seems to remember, the writer or artist abandons herself to ethical quicksand. In cutting off the thing represented – in this case the life of Caslon – from the thing itself, one appropriates that thing while at the same time, in the same wrenching gesture of detachment, divesting it of all reality, thereby rendering the thing a fake. An artist's fantasy. Maybe this comes to mind at this instance when their bodies are hurtling through space in a metal and glass box, her feet wedged between the car door and a plastic gas can and some yellowed newspapers, because she has seen in his face a look she recognizes that she herself has felt. Caslon leans forward on the vinyl bench seat, turning off his cellphone, and Etti sees dissatisfaction – a very particular dissatisfaction that comes from drifting out of the present and looking upon oneself at a distance.

In seeing this vulnerable side of Caslon, she wonders if there is any way to do what she's been tasked with without forming a bond with her subject. How could she do this without starting to love the man, in the way that she often began to love the teens she worked with? How else could she maintain such fidelity to him?

An afternoon driving the streets, riding in the back seats of Ladas, what must be some kind of informal underground taxi service, Caslon on his cellphone or gazing out his side window. At stops he buzzes at intercoms and enters stairwells and apartments, greeting men heartily, those men often looking a little perplexed at his arrival, only to exchange a few back-and-forths. Twice he stays for a sip of tea before departing, and every time he meets someone they seem to know in advance not to acknowledge Etti's presence. With a forced blank expression on her face, an expression that in seeking neutrality likely betrays some degree of apprehension to those present, Etti stands a few feet away – as though, she begins to think, I'm a few seconds behind Caslon. In most cases the men can't help but look at her in passing, and she wonders if they are more curious about what she is doing by Caslon's side, or how she looks in doing it.

The taxi pulls to the side of the road and Caslon pays the driver and gets out again, goes directly to the intercom built into an iron gate and punches through the listing until the name comes up that he's looking for. A buzz and Caslon enters the courtyard, Etti close behind, the courtyard dim in the overcast evening, then into a bunker-like stairwell with open-air windows, through another door to a hallway and to an apartment door. The man on the other side is friendly, and his apartment is modern and almost empty except for large colour photos on the walls. Like the other meetings, Caslon's acquaintance seems perplexed at first and then things shift to a kind of normal, and the meeting is brief. Caslon seems more relaxed after he leaves this apartment, more satisfied. Though she has no idea what's been exchanged, Etti detects the exact second in their conversation that Caslon's attitude lightens.

They enter a multi-level bookstore full of light and cool air. She follows Caslon to the second floor, past reproductions of Soviet propaganda posters with happy and enfranchised labourers, women and men, sleeves rolled up, and she observes him as he scans the shelves. It's a bilingual bookstore, English and Russian titles. They are in philosophy, and then in fiction, then in art and poetry. Caslon seems purposefully to hide the books that he pulls from the shelf, and at the sales counter, though she is able to see them, she wonders if she is not supposed to, and tries to assemble a connection between the titles that he's picked out. The ten books that he will end up stacking at his beside table and flipping through one morning or afternoon at the hotel, or in the evening after they have come back from the club, after a young prostitute has left the room, glancing at the odd paragraph or inspecting the bibliographies or indexes or content pages but never reading two pages in succession, and looking somewhat frustrated, as though he wants to be absorbed in them but cannot find an entry point.

A block away from their hotel, a black SUV collides with their cab, sending them up a small embankment into a wall. Everyone from the two cars gets out – the taxi driver, Etti and Caslon, and two men from the black Mercedes. Though she had not been paying attention to the road from the back seat, she surely senses that the Mercedes has caused the collision – they hadn't swerved out of their lane – but Etti doubts the men will agree that they are at fault, given that one of them is already pointing his finger at Etti, who stands at her now-established position a few feet to the side and back from Caslon. They come closer and utter a string of words, and she absorbs the words since they are directed at her, doing the best she can to act as though she is not there. Her heart rate skyrockets, perhaps less from the possibility of violence than from the seeming injustice of what's unfolding, wondering why they have singled her out since she has clearly come out of the back seat of the car, never mind that it was the SUV that crossed lanes. She keeps expecting Caslon to intervene, but he stands in place even as one of the men reaches out and squeezes her chin between his thumb and forefinger. Etti observes Caslon as she suffers the man's shouts, and Caslon, whom everyone surely anticipates to make the next move, lets the men inch closer. The scene slows until it is almost frozen in time. Then, as though it only just occurs to him, Caslon turns away from the men, leaves Etti, and heads back to the Lada. Etti can do nothing but pull her face from the man's grip and follow. Caslon retrieves his plastic bag full of new books from the car, goes over to the cab driver who has turned away from his smoking wreck, away from the whole scene, and is staring hopelessly past the wall at the canal, and hands him a wad of cash. He returns to the two men, whose heads look like they are about to explode, and hands the most aggressive of the two what looks like a business card, and without saying anything, turns and crosses to the opposite sidewalk. Etti follows behind him, not turning to see the scene they have left in pieces until Caslon himself turns to take it in, smiling before continuing on his way.

Victoria

The two who came in masks: it had been so long since I witnessed negotiation conducted with such hushed focus, it felt like a lifetime ago. From a shared commiseration over Victoria, concern over her physical state, to a cerebral exchange that entirely excluded us, on it went, subtly ebbing then intensifying. The quality of their pauses made it seem they were not anticipating each other's thoughts, that they were surprising each other, pushing their back-and-forth to another level, that they were continuously responding to what the other said as if no position could hold beyond the present articulation, the length of time it took to register meaning. Delight might also have been expressed, maybe even love – I say this even though all I could hear was muffled speech without the distinctness of individual words. All I could see was the paper mask covering each of their faces. Their heights were equal, like twins, and I could easily tell that one was a man and one a woman. The man's mask was a moon-face, round, gently curved at the front and irregularly dimpled, and the woman's was smooth and heart-shaped like a martian.

They were like seasoned lovers that still could really do it for each other, it seemed to me. Not at all twins, but lovers.

For whatever reason, they feel it necessary to haul Victoria out of her condo with firm precise grips on her arms, careful not to hurt her even as she drags her dead weight between them. She is lifted into the back of an empty white van where the moon man continues to hold her, the woman martian climbing up front to the driver's seat. Victoria says nothing the whole time.

They take her to a warehouse loft that at one time would have been common in the city, the kind Etti and I used to frequent over a decade ago for parties. This one, adrift from the percep-tible march of time, feels elite for its scarcity, like it shouldn't exist at all now. Or maybe not elite, maybe left behind, the world having moved on without it.

Inside their loft they strap Victoria to a turquoise bucket chair, leaving her as they retreat to a corner of the room. They talk in a tone so uniformly low that I can't make out any words. The flat of the white full-moon face brushes against the tapered martian ear, and I am able to see the side of the moon man's face, several days stubble marking his cheek. They drift and get sidetracked, then proceed with an even-paced dialogue. They look upon each other through their little eye-holes, perhaps in disagreement, but more likely to consider what the other has said. The woman martian finally raises the level of her voice:

Yes, she says and disappears from sight into another room. The moon man stands where he is in the corner, hands resting on his hips as though still mulling over their decision.

The warehouse room is expansive, filled with tree-sized plants and mid-century modern chairs, some residual objects from earlier in the century and others from the '80s. The moon man really inhabits the room, naturally belonging to the furniture and old crossbeams. I can't help but wonder, as they begin their operation, exactly how old they are. My faith in them hinges on that age, I realize. If they are younger than me, I think, we are doomed.

The woman martian comes back with a cardboard box from which she removes an extension cord and an aluminum clip-on lamp and plugs them together so that a light comes on. She points it away from Victoria and waits. Meanwhile the moon man leaves and returns, attempting to tear a tea towel in half lengthwise, what looks like stained Marimekko flowers decorating the linen. He steps behind Victoria to tie one half around her eyes, and it's not long enough, so he ties on the other half. Victoria does nothing.

The woman martian takes the moon man aside, and after words are exchanged, returns to Victoria and removes the tea-towel blind, leaves and comes back with a glass of water for Victoria. The woman martian points the light at Victoria, holding it still, then swivels it up and down her body. As the woman martian makes an adjustment to the lamp, I fly everywhere, over plants and across the high wooden ceiling.

The moon man draws the curtains to close off the last light of day and retrieves dark sheets from somewhere to peg on as another layer.

Finally the woman martian speaks. She looks deeply into Victoria's eyes and says, We are going to free you. She sounds confident, deliberate in her choice of words. She has a soothing voice that still leaves something up to the listener. I can't help but feel that she's speaking directly to me.

The woman martian clips the lamp high on a bookshelf, pointing it down at Victoria, and I fall to the grain of the wood floor, across dust and crumbs. Already the woman martian is kneeling above me, placing her hands on my shadow self, and I fall over the back of her hands. The moon man joins in, but neither can touch me without my darkness draping their search. They pat the floor methodically, patiently, without any sense that time is bearing down.

Another quick conference in the corner, then the woman martian unties Victoria and stands her up. She holds Victoria's waist while the moon man begins manipulating her body. Arms up, arms at the side. I form different shapes on the wall and floor. The woman martian orbits the lamplight around Victoria, projecting me on the wall, a face-on view over a large painting and then a side view across the spines of LPs at the far end of the room, then a stretch along the floor, up the wall before expanding to the ceiling, over the old-growth beams. I'm used to being projected as Victoria moves about the world catching stable points of light – the bright sun and diffuse office lights and table lamps – but these experiments put me on display, making me self-conscious.

While I lie flat on one wall, finally still, the woman martian comes to me. She puts her masked lips where mine would have been, waits, then blows air through a small cutout as though down into my lungs. The moon man watches, toggling a lamp switch on and off several times. He changes the pattern as though performing Morse code, with longer and shorter periods of darkness and light. He adds more lights at various angles, now leaving them all on, peeling me out spirographically. Then, perhaps inspired by that effect, he adds more lights. He keeps adding with greater momentum, illuminating the room like a world's fair. I feel fainter and fainter, fading in stark contrast to Victoria's intensifying whiteness, and I think, they are achieving what they wanted, I am really disappearing. My point on the grid is under absolute erasure. Then at the very brink, as the nausea recedes from Victoria and the glow of life returns to her, I think, ah fuck, these two young people have really done it.

The last thing I see is the moon man step forward, and for just a moment, lift his mask. Though the lights that surround us all are blinding, I do see that bright face, that smooth forehead and even stubble. Those eyes that have only seen twenty-five or so years. I see him looking at Victoria in triumph before his mask falls back over his face, and then I see nothing. I know nothing.

Then I hear Victoria gasp 'no!' and the moon man say 'the

156

circuit breaker' and the room appears again in darkness. The woman martian cleans up the floor in front of Victoria, who is squatting in distress. The moon man mumbles, It was not sustainable.

For the first time I notice, in another dark corner of the room, a tripod and camera, green light on.

Victoria breaks the silence and asks, quietly, Are you Jan Melbrooks? Moon face, are you Melbrooks?

The moon man turns his head to her.

Or were you sent by Jan Melbrooks? she asks. Or Said?

The moon man and the woman martian retreat to the corner of the room, by the video camera, and talk on and on, perhaps for longer than any previous discussion. When finally they pull out of their discourse, the woman martian says: I suppose it does matter who we are, but you don't need to know our names. We are not Said or Melbrooks. We are other people. We want to help you, but we want to learn from helping you. Your situation speaks to us. We want to know what an error like the one you're enduring looks like. We're fascinated by it because it seems emblematic of something greater.

I don't care about being emblematic, Victoria says. I don't care about your fascination.

Across the darkness they stare at Victoria as though she's a painting they've been working on, as though something is off that they can't determine. The woman martian rests her arm over the moon man's shoulders.

That night they keep us captive in their loft. Victoria helps the woman martian pull out a futon mattress while the moon man paces in another room. He comes out into the living room to see how the futon is coming along, a worn orange and black trade paperback in his hand, his finger marking a page. I see myself in him, am willing to believe the answer will come from a book. I want to believe that words from a book could unravel our situation. Maybe theory about the way people interact and the way the economy dictates social relations. If enough is known about our situation, I think, perhaps he will be able to release me from Victoria. But another part of me knows that such a book would have no answer. Rather it would simply present the contradictions by which we live our lives, offering no solutions or even consolations, just ways that someone might constantly interrogate them, and because this truth is stronger than blind faith, I know that the moon man and the martian woman will fail. This recognition makes me feel the years separating me from the moon man, who certainly believes in the object that he holds far more than what I could now.

When he shifts the book to his other hand I can see part of the title written in white over a giant black '1.' It is familiar to me. I've seen it a number of times over the course of my life. Growing up, I saw it on the shelves of parents, but like most of those books never gave it much thought. It was just a spine among so many others. And when I was older I would see it in the philosophy section of used bookstores, its title radiating another era, my parents' era. I would leave it on those shelves unopened. I might never have thought of it again in my entire life had the moon man not revealed it as he changed his grip: *One-Dimensional Man*. It makes me reel. Could there be any relationship between me and that title character? I mean, the obvious one? The moon man looks the portrait of ineffectuality standing absolutely still with that book in his hand, finger sandwiched in its pages, his round face overseeing Victoria and the woman martian as they finish with the pillowcases. At least that is how I see him. Things could not be worse.

Victoria stirs very early, but I have been up for some time, trying to clear my mind of the moon man and his book. I try to imagine the face of the woman martian, her eyes, her mouth. She is the only bright light in the room.

The more the couple had conferred, the more I found the woman martian to be so perfect. I couldn't keep my eyes off of her. I could watch the two of them for hours because of the way they were with each other, because of how she was with him. Sometime during their low-voiced negotiations it hit me how much I desired not just to work alongside the two of them, but to be that moon man, flat moon face against the heart-shaped martian cheeks. There was nothing about their situation that I did not want.

Before bed, they took a few flash photos of Victoria, and as the blasts of light burnt into our eyes I was certain that the solution to Victoria and me was so far beyond emblems. It had to be a light from the future that would obliterate the shadows, that would destroy the very idea of job shadowing along with whatever job shadowing actually signified.

But what this light looked like, what it was, whether it was at all possible, I had no idea. I kept thinking about it as though I would be able to conjure that light. I tried to be optimistic. I tried to really believe that something exceeding me would change and send a light my way.

And then I remembered: *It is strange that when we are children a lot of things are there and were there before we were born. But we assume a more extreme version of this, an absolute version of this: that those things were always there, way back into the past, when in fact they happened just ten, maybe five years before we were born. Perhaps JFK was shot the year before you were born, or perhaps the Beatles broke up on the day that you were born. For you, this is in the infinite past, and remains just as one more fact of the way the world is. It is not until you are much older that you realize the proximity of your life to things that happened before you were born. Even though your parents' bookshelves may be lined with books about the JFK assassination or with books about the Challenger disaster or Chernobyl or the Berlin Wall coming down, books that were always on their shelves ever since you were born, you still relegate it all to a permanent past, and you can't even imagine that these things happened at the threshold of your birth, that your parents and millions of other parents lived through them and were affected enough to buy books about them. All we see of our parents are Mom and Dad, not participants in whatever else was going on* in the world. We see them as they are in the present, and we see their objects as things from a past that is fixed in stone. And we see ourselves projected into the future as what we want to be when we grow up, because what we are now is not what we are, is not what we will become. That is what it is like to be a child, and that is what it is like to be a teenager.

As we go along, getting older, we begin to see that the past casts a long shadow over the present, that the things that were always there before we were born are still there, but that they're not inert like chunks of concrete. We see that there is a powerful light behind all of the objects of the past, and that this light blasts into those objects, forging long shadows into the present and into the future. And we see that these shadows are more than just shadows. Some of them are like glue and some of them are quicksand, and some of them are vacuums that suck all the meaning out of life. Not to get too dramatic, but so much is at stake here.

What is that light?

Jan Melbrooks threw it out to the audience without an answer, as though it was our task to unveil that light for ourselves. As though the very purpose of the job shadowing would be to locate the source of that past light. But the way he said it, the smile that went along with it, suggested, almost imperceptibly, that he found it funny. If there was a single moment when he seemed to be pulling something over on us, it was then. It lasted for a fraction of a second, a hiccup so brief that the audience might have doubted it ever happened. But it did. At least I saw it happen.

Effectively disrupting the silent morning rays streaming in among overgrown potted plants, vines and ferns, glassware and silkscreened rock posters – a creaturely accumulation that makes the couple seem all that much more at ease in the world – Victoria begins speaking. She focuses on a point between the moon man and the woman martian, either the nothingness of air itself or the black and white photo on the wall behind them, what looks like businessmen reaching out to shake each other's hands. She says:

You seem to believe you can outthink my situation. I can see you aren't stupid, or bad, but I can also see from yesterday's blunders that you're misguided. Your ways don't seem to apply. I look at this place that you live in and think, what the fuck are you doing? I don't relate.

Still, even as you shone your cheap lamps around, I felt something good towards you. It took me a lot of thinking about myself last night to understand this. A lot of reflection. I'm no longer 20. I'm 23. I'm more self-aware. You made me feel totally different from how I feel at work. At work I often feel nothing at all, or I feel blah. I know that anyone else could do what I'm doing. And my bosses, while they know that I could do a lot more, don't care to give me a chance. But their attitudes alone shouldn't cause me to feel so pointless. Who cares if anyone could do the job? That doesn't mean it should be an empty experience. We could celebrate the fact that anyone could do the job. But of course I want more. I've built my life through exercises and schooling and doing things. I have skills that I want to use.

I've heard that the larger an organization is, the more specialized the jobs are, and the less chance you have to do anything outside your narrow job description. Maybe this is one reason why I said yes to the job shadowing, in order to do something outside of my job description. And I felt some pressure from above. I don't know if it was really there or just imagined. I lost sleep over making the decision, which I realized was really no decision at all. The first time I met Said – who I assume you actually do know – he said there was an opportunity that had come up that I might be interested in, that might benefit me. Not that it would make me rise in the organization, but rather that it would ensure I got to stay there longer, that it would give me more time. It would show my manager that I was willing. And I *was* willing. One thing you have to do to keep your job is to please at all costs. So I accepted it, believing a young woman would be attached to me. That's what was set up for me, or so I believed.

But then, in the conference hall, I glanced over at him a few times as the speaker was onstage. His behaviour irritated me, so I kept looking over at him. He was distracted, looking around and not really noticing me sitting right beside him. I didn't know he was assigned to me – I thought the person on my other side, a woman of my age, was my assignment, and it was only when that woman didn't disappear, and he *did* disappear, that I understood what had happened. But how was I to believe this? What evidence did I have other than his disappearance? I looked around the room and people had disappeared all over the place. But what was I supposed to think?

I realize now that I have made a major mistake. I was naive with the shadowing. Always saying yes is naive. Despite how

163

crappy I must look to you now, I'm trying to build an image. I'm working on a unique skillset. I'm aiming to be invaluable, irreplaceable. I mean, I'm doing everything right. The shadow has destroyed all these possibilities for me.

Victoria is almost in tears. So that is my story. What are you going to do for me?

There is silence in the kitchen before the moon man says, We think you should stay with us for a while. This is partly in your hands, but there is also space for others to help. We can look after you, he says.

Yesterday we were testing the physicality of the shadow phenomenon, the woman martian says. We believe that the physical body has a role in all this. There must be other forces at play too.

To begin, we need one thing from you, Victoria, the moon man says. We need you to see that this is not inevitable, that it's not normal. If I can convey a single thing, let it be this. You have to see that it could be otherwise.

Fine, she says. I know that.

Okay. Another thing too, the moon man continues. You see Victoria, there might be something good for you in having this man as your shadow. At the moment you started to accept and recognize his presence, did you not start seeing the world, the whole of your existence, afresh? So that now your job was no longer the same job, but an apparatus for using up your days.

That it had, in fact, entirely overtaken your life while giving you almost nothing in return. Surely the shadowing has allowed you to see the job for what it is. And it has allowed you to see reality beyond Learning Ecologies. So while you want him gone, you might also thank him.

Victoria stands as though to leave.

Hold on, the woman martian says. Don't go yet. There is truth to what he has just told you. I mean, how can you deny that your world has shifted on its axis, and that –

Victoria begins walking to the door.

Hold on, the woman martian says again with her soothing voice. Someone spoke to us about your circumstance, she says. She was a shadow too, but something didn't gel for her. She was assigned to a man about her own age. He had a family and worked fairly high-up in the organization. But something was not right. The shadowing barely started before ending, and it's not entirely clear why it fell apart. They both seemed happy to be doing it. More willing than most. What we do know is that the shadowing woman spoke to the man before the transformation, at the table in the conference centre. They seemed to get along. But it is likely that something about this contact and the words that passed between them doomed their shadowing. Perhaps they recognized something in each other that disabled the shadowing. Perhaps they exchanged something that undercut the whole process, despite all their willingness.

Now the woman martian stares hard at Victoria, straight

through her pupils. Maybe this needs to be said to you, Shadow, more than Victoria: when I mentioned other forces at work, what I meant was, in addition to all of the worldly forces, the economy and history and so forth, there is also some individual force of energy that has a tremendous effect on others. That is for you to think about.

The moon man sits back without stepping in. He opens up *One-Dimensional Man*, which has been sitting on the table the whole time, pulls out a rolled joint that's replaced his finger as a bookmark, lights it, takes it behind his mask to get it going, and holds it in the air for Victoria. She gives him a look of distain.

How about you, Shadow? he says, and keeps the joint in the air.

Finally, the woman martian says, We are not going to make you stay here, Victoria. We will not keep you here against your will. But we highly recommend you stay until we can understand everything better.

Don't you see, Victoria says as she tries the locked door handle, that I don't have much faith in your abilities, even if you are all that I've got. If I've learned anything from you it's that I need to do this on my own.

Etti

For the rest of the day, Etti remains shaken by the accident, wondering if she will have to sustain more violence, and having no idea what direction it might come from. Caslon seems to have taken it all in stride, even enjoying its energy, and since she is preoccupied by his strange reaction, she too goes with it.

Now observing Caslon search through a rack of elegant dresses at the mall where they'd opened her bank account, she notices a young shop woman approach. Caslon exchanges words with her. He puts a few dresses aside and the shop woman looks Etti up and down and pulls out one of the dresses, maybe in a smaller size. It is silver and well formed. Etti is uncertain whether she should take this dress into the change room, because the dress is surely for her, and the situation of fitting clothes seems an exception to the rhythm they've slipped into. Caslon gives her no indication, and again says something to the woman and the woman takes the silver dress away to the counter, boxing it up while Caslon pays for it with his card.

In another shop, following an exchange similar to the one in the dress shop, Caslon purchases high-heeled shoes, black with dark-purple soles, and a small silver clutch.

She does nothing to her near-black hair other than washing it while he is napping. She lets it drape behind her ears, parted at the side as it always is. He wears expensive pants and a shirt with the sleeves rolled up. He looks himself, and she looks like someone else in the new dress and shoes. They almost look like a plausible couple. It is warm out as they walk a little way from the hotel and wait for a car to arrive and take them away. They cross the river for the first time since their arrival, a wide river with long flat party boats streaming in both directions, and on its far bank, in this more isolated part of the city, they are dropped off by a large courtyard. People are gathered inside, cigarette smoking and drinking wine from real glasses, everyone elegantly dressed, men in black and women in pinks and reds and greens. Looks pass between Caslon and the partyers before they enter through the wide-open doors of the gallery. Etti likely notices the decorative plaster edging the ceiling, painted gold and white, and the chandeliers and other moulded details around every door frame, long velvet curtains covering massive windows, all in contrast to the images installed on the the walls, which, at least from Etti's point of view, seem to be from the last ten or so years, though they could be from last week, or even this morning.

This room of the gallery is already very crowded, and Etti is forced right up against her subject, shoulder to shoulder, making it a challenge to maintain his perspective as he surveys the room. When a man approaches Caslon, he naturally believes Etti is with him, and he speaks to Caslon in English: Caslon, he says. Man, who is this catch? looking straight at Etti. Caslon says that she is not to be noted, and the man doesn't respond other than to glance once more at her. The man begins talking about his new yacht, how it was built by a company specializing in sustainable materials, how it is powered by the water itself. It's kind of a test model, he says. Exceptionally slow moving. And he glances again at Etti.

Present and absent at the same time. A medium for Caslon's memoir. She certainly hasn't been transparent – people cannot help but see her, to stare a little. They must wonder why it is that she's attached to Caslon. Why, given all his power and wealth, he's chosen someone like her: verging on forty, not stunning though interesting looking, large eyes, medium-dark skin tone, black hair with heavier eyebrows. Why he has chosen someone who seems, while attentive and intelligent, somewhat strange.

Perhaps they try to relate her to people they know, and failing, see her as nothing more than one of Caslon's unpredictable diversions – a woman who could in fact be a lover if he were in one of his moods, dipping among the masses, looking for a reality not available to him on the yacht. Someone with the smell of another reality. And in this they would be partly right. But more likely they would see her for her nameable differences, her alien qualities, as representative of some other world that did not share the same reference points. A lower world, one guided by principles that they themselves would happily discount or altogether banish from their busy days. Etti does not know. Even with them, she tries to remain open.

She gathers from the eco-yacht owner that what surrounds them in the gallery is exclusively the work of yacht owners, that there is an art club among what must be an elite international yacht association. On one wall she's able to see a series of photos depicting human-damaged landscapes – images that have become so popular in the photo world, she likely thinks, the earth altered at a geological level. A documentary look, melancholy or pessimistic even when a lush forest is depicted.

The man asks about Caslon's work. Where is it? he asks. I want to see it. You'll have to find it for yourself, Caslon says, and the man takes the opportunity to exit their conversation. Caslon and Etti begin to make a round of the gallery, Caslon spending as much time inspecting the labels as looking at the photos and drawings themselves. They drift through the rooms, on and on, taking in a lot of nautical-themed art – ropes and fittings and seascapes. Surely a few of the attendees are Caslon's associates, Etti thinks, but he avoids contact with everyone. After they have travelled the periphery of several rooms, they come to them, what Caslon must be looking for: a series of medium-sized photos. Caslon chuckles and shakes his head a little, and Etti tries to understand exactly what he is experiencing, though it is impossible for her to gather beyond his recognition of something. But this in itself is significant, she must think, it is not simply recognition; he is surprised at the work.

Caslon goes to the start of the series. The first image is a typical party snapshot, with Caslon posing alongside others who all look drunk, he in the centre and a couple of men and women on either side, crowding in. He pauses on the image. Etti sees right away that the face is slightly off, that it must be the other Caslon. The next image is a black and white still, what looks like the American moon landing, empty of figures. The next is another party snapshot, a selfie with all of the flush, damp party faces leaning in together – again the other Caslon. The next is a video of Zidane's head-butt playing in a quick loop on a screen equal in size to the still images. Then another party shot of the other Caslon pointing at the camera, a tumbler and cigarette in his hand. The next is a black and white photo of a man with a sullen face, a heavy moustache, hair parted in the centre. Then Caslon's second again, this time with a woman on his lap, clothed but from her posture seemingly mid-coitus, perhaps faking it for the photo but perhaps not. The next makes Caslon laugh out loud: a photo of the car crash with Etti face to face with the driver or passenger of the other car, Caslon at her side, the crashed Lada in the background. Caslon can hardly contain himself, so funny it is to him. The final work in the series is another mid-sized screen, but the screen is dead. The label beside this one – the label for the entire series – reads *Independence,* or *The Beautiful Convergence of a Man with his Analogue.* An asterisked sentence below reads *Live feed still to come!*

A voice comes over a speaker system – an announcement in Russian – and Caslon makes his way back through the galleries to where people are congregating. The voice sounds again and eventually everyone arranges themselves, and a woman appears at a podium. Though Etti doesn't know the language, she assumes the woman begins by thanking people, corporate sponsors, and the audience does clap after she lists a few names. Caslon scans the faces in the crowd, and many of those faces are also glancing around.

It is into this proper moment, this moment that is repeated all over the world whenever artists are in debt and need to demonstrate their gratitude to sponsors, even in this exceptional case when all the artists presumably have all the money in the world, that the other Caslon enters. His face is flush with victory, childish in its unabashed glory. His hands might as well be raised skyward, so self-evident he must believe his victory is to anyone watching. As much as Etti has entered Caslon's life and become attached to him, seeing the world from his point of view, she can't help but feel a little tug for this second iteration, his juvenile energy, brought into the world fully formed with such impossible expectations put on him. She wonders how it must feel for this man, having lost fraternity with his original self, becoming his employee and ultimately, it seems to her now as they gaze at each other across the room, his antagonist.

Caslon himself maintains a neutral expression. He appears ready for whatever will happen. Etti knows that nothing good can come of this meeting. Two things that are almost the same do not open up much of a space, or only open up a space that will close in a violent collision. She imagines an event more violent than what she already witnessed between them, far more theatrical because of the audience, and loaded with the new meaning that a gallery setting would force upon it. And, she realizes, thinking of the asterisked label, someone must have turned on a video camera by now.

By the time the woman has ended her speech, the two Caslons are staring each other down. They begin walking toward each other with a visible symmetry. The room is loud again with chatter and some attendees are already dispersing. But some hang on, watching the doubles and Etti cross the room, the gap closing as though they might walk into each other and become one. Caslon's face is no longer neutral but wide-eyed, smiling in anticipation.

When they stop, the second is face to face with Etti, who rather than meeting his eyes keeps watch over Caslon, who himself is staring at his second, the three of them triangulating their gazes. The second Caslon says to Etti: You...

And Caslon steps in to tell him to stop talking to her, and he continues to Etti: You are here, of course.

Caslon places his hand flat against the second's chest, and the second continues: You should have come back to talk to me at the party. I wanted to know more about you. The fish wanted to know more. And Caslon grabs him by the collar and the second grabs Etti, and the three of them stumble their way out of the gallery, past all the gallery-goers through the courtyard to the sidewalk. They get caught up in one another's legs and trip down the street, like drunks arm in arm. Someone is steering them, or all three of them are steering one another down a sloped street, which leads them toward the river where the light standards indicate the start of the bridge, the second meanwhile shouting: You don't really believe in this...

Caslon says nothing in response, and Etti, watching his face, wonders if he wants to hear what his second has to say.

The second Caslon says to Etti: They listen to him when he says you're not there. But you are there so that he is fully there.

Her Caslon is grabbing at the second Caslon's throat now.

Even as she is dragged along by the second Caslon, watching Caslon squeeze the other man's throat, Etti thinks of her dear friend F. She confesses that she might have bought into the idea that she's not there. But sometimes you need to buy into something false in order to make something happen, she says to F. Isn't that true?

They reach a low cement barrier at the edge of the river, stumbling among promenaders and drunks and youth dressed in ballgowns and suits. Flashes go off from cellphone cameras. The world spinning around Etti looks so festive, all lights against darkness.

Look at him, the second says, he wants something that money can't buy. The moment I came into this world he tried to – and Caslon is really squeezing his throat now – differentiate himself from me. Even though he wanted a double-life . . . he couldn't help but . . . want to be different from that second life. . . Tell me . . . what do you think of yourself in all this?

He keeps going despite the grip on his throat: It must be like watching TV for you, he says. Something that starts off good but then . . . becomes repetitive . . . until it becomes an embarrassing waste of time . . . Formulas forever reborn by fake conflicts. Doesn't that . . . summarize Caslon for us?

Etti is thrown free of the second Caslon's grasp, falling to the sidewalk, and the two men grapple against the waist-high bridge wall below which the river continues its flush toward the Bay of Finland. The last thing that comes from the second's mouth is, Time to turn it off!

As the men wrestle their way across the bridge, further and further from her, she wonders if her own unity with Caslon is dependent on his obsession with this third figure – his double. Where would they be without this focal point? He would not know what to do with himself. But then she wonders instead whether the task of witnessing Caslon's life alone binds them. Whether in itself it is enough. She knows it is not like a TV series for her, as the second has claimed. She does grow closer to Caslon the more she watches him, not farther away. It becomes less like watching.

Moreover, she thinks, am I not in some way the author of this? Of this very scene? Am I not the author of this, F? It is a perverse thought, but somehow true to her. How can it be like watching TV when I am the author of it?

More, F says to her. One step further.

What do you mean? Etti says.

One step beyond authoring him. Are you not the actual representation of him? Isn't this the truest sense of this scenario? You as his representational image?

And Etti shakes F from her mind. She becomes heavy with both the men. The second Caslon's lack of independence grows more and more unjust in her mind. Like I am fighting that man, she thinks.

In the corner of her vision she spots, inches from her hand, perched on the river wall, a ballpoint pen. She grabs it without a second thought. She puts it into her silver clutch, which has become completely crumpled in her grip.

When she looks up, the men are farther away, fighting amid the traffic on the bridge. There could not be a more opportune time to escape. But she keeps to her task of watching. Or authoring. She is there to see one of the men toss the other into the river.

Victoria

We are on her balcony for the first time since I have become part of her. I have no idea how serious she is about throwing herself off, onto the street furniture below, but she has indicated her intent.

Something has changed with her proposal of suicide. She speaks to me now, opening her mouth to me, letting the shaped air come out, which she has never done before. In all these weeks that I've been with her, all she has ever done is yell profanities at me. Now, if I could respond, I would say, Victoria, please don't throw yourself off the balcony. We will figure this out. Together we can do this.

She's not the suicidal type. Everything is about a planned future in which she is farther along than she is now. And though she is desperate or resigned to giving up, surely she still believes there is a way out somewhere in front of her. That she can save herself through applying her skills. I know that she can picture herself in the future, in control of her employment situation – I know this must be true. Maybe with her own website that shows off what she can do. Already she has chosen a particular font for her name and a tag line for her emails. She surely has faith in success through individual application. The story of success is being able to picture that future self. Speculation in the self. Perhaps that is what I've taken away from her. But perhaps that is also the very thing that was taken away from all the job shadowers.

Leaning at the edge, she says, I have no idea why anyone would want you to shadow in the first place. As a shadow you are of no value whatsoever to anyone. If you were simply unemployed you would apply to jobs, be part of a competition that is essential to it all working. But as a shadow you are removed altogether from that competition. You are no good to the economy or to me or yourself. She sighs as though everything that has come out of her mouth is pointless. What the hell is all this for?

We will figure this out, I want to say to her. But the truth is I have no idea how to talk to her.

We lived quietly with her illness in the short period after leaving the moon man and the woman martian. I could not stop thinking about them, their warehouse space and their way of being together. It did not matter to me who they were, but rather that they lived in what looked like beautiful and mercurial equality. Perhaps because of their differences of opinion they had grown equal together. And I could not stop thinking about the way they inhabited their space as though it was an extension of themselves. Delving into their world had unlocked so many things I desired, a world that I recognized, that had trawled through the material history of earlier generations. In my heart there was still a vestige of youthful entelechy from my early twenties. This romance demanded a phantasmagoria of dated objects, an apartment that doubled as a cabinet of cultural highlights. A turntable with Sun Ra and Stevie Wonder spinning on it, Prestige and ESP and Impulse jazz. I desired an ever-increasing library, Lustig- and Kuhlman-designed books lining Dieter Rams shelving. Tapio Wirkkala and Kaj Franck glasses, Marcel Breuer chairs and Eames coat hangers, an arc floor lamp and Dainolite table lamps, long studio desks propped up with two-by-fours. Linen upholstery. Teak everywhere. An IBM wall clock like they have in new city hall. Objects into which designers had poured social ideals that reflected a new way of life. A whole way of being that assumed a rich interplay of a private life and open doors. All those books and records and prints and glasses from the past did not cast a shadow over my twenty-year-old self as they did now. But I still desired them. Because if all this material wealth were true, surely all else was well. Surely in this future among these objects I was a professional of some kind, comfortably bringing in money. I was looked upon by colleagues and friends with respect and admiration.

As we were leaving, it was the woman martian that led us out to the warehouse elevator. In what she whispered to Victoria, there was such an echo of Josephine I was set off-balance. She

179

must have been addressing me when she said: Nostalgia for what your parents had can be nothing more than a desire for power. The freedom you imagine those fatherly men to have had was nothing but a position of power above so many others.

One always seeks the day on which an event takes place that changes the way we are. One always seeks the original event even if it never transpired. We know that there are only earlier and later iterations of the phenomenon, never a first one. And those iterations are so naturalized, so easy to miss.

It occurs to me that I know nothing about the history of job shadowing. I wonder if anyone does.

I imagine myself from the outside, as the author of this history: a man sliding into middle age, consumed by the idea that would surely lead to the depths of his parents' generation, perhaps reaching back before them. That man gains satisfaction from uncovering all of the good intentions of the job shadowing founders before, years passing, their ideals are lost to programs of shadowing done unthinkingly. Before the practice becomes institutionalized. I see him putting his discoveries into a theoretical framework, meanwhile scrambling to make a name for himself in the process, so that he shapes an academic career from his diligence and burgeoning authority. The resulting book would slip into the long list of history-of books – walking, and violence, money, shit, writing, and tears, debt, and so forth. And that would satisfy him.

The idea clings to me, though I know I will never do it. Even though it is imaginary, it becomes the point on the horizon that has been so evasive.

Victoria sits in the corner of the balcony against a glass panel, which provides no shade against the direct sunlight. She's stopped talking. I persist in trying to speak to her. I tell her about the history of job shadowing, which I will never write, but which I will keep thinking about for weeks or months.

In junior high school, I tell her, I was a shadow for a day. I chose to follow a colleague of my father around at his workplace, at the university. I don't remember anything of the experience except what we were told by our teacher in the classroom: Never ask someone how much they make. I took such things so seriously back then. I didn't question the teacher and I didn't ask the man what he made. I took it as the fundamental prohibition of shadowing. Never ask someone how much money they make.

But on the condo's balcony it seems like exactly what I need to do. How much money do you make? I ask Victoria. Tell me, how much? There is nothing special in my delivery that would allow her to hear me, but I try a number of times. I hound her over it. How much do you make, Victoria? And perhaps there is a minimal difference in the way I ask her now than how I might have in the past. I try to ask out loud rather than imagining asking her. I vocalize it.

That's not even the question, she shouts back at me.

And something is changing in me.

That's not even our question now. There's nothing out there! she shouts. There's nothing out there.

And she is saying it directly to me, because I am now standing before her.

Etti

In the enclosure where the furniture of the motorboat curves out of the hull, she sits blindfolded in silver, out on the water in a gentle sway and drift, Caslon having cut the motor a minute ago. They are at recess.

She finds freedom in blindness. Her mind locates a territory of emptiness far from the noise of ideas and the discourses with F, ideal like photos of landscapes or abandoned buildings or abandoned industrial complexes.

It's not long before Caslon sighs, unable to let the silence last, unwilling to let their communing be ended. This was bound to happen, he says. And while it may have been inevitable, he continues, it's still a problem. Etti?

That empty space away from Caslon was a fantasy, she thinks, but it leaves her with the thought: had her memoirizing ever transformed into anything beyond work? She is exhausted by the intensity of Caslon's life but also knows that exhaustion can clear the emotions, removing all the crap to get at purer existence. Had a kind of love formed out of their unwavering intimacy? When one puts so much into someone else, it is hard for love not to form. She's not read this anywhere, but it seems true to her. Working with teens has taught her this. And now. Her efforts had led her in that direction, but surely, following the incident with his manufactured double, those feelings that might have been love have become tenuous.

I can't be found dead in a river, Caslon says. I can't be found dead in that gush of water and then be spotted hanging around at a party among the living. I also can't show up in some video post, grappling with myself through the city.

In his voice she hears melancholy, even regret. She's never heard him like this before. It doesn't suit him. There's a charge underlying it that makes it feel off, disingenuous – as though in his remorse he's nevertheless invigorated by what has happened. A double feeling that he doesn't know how to handle, that he isn't capable of handling. Still, Etti becomes appropriately serious to his mood. She agrees that he should not be alive and dead at the same time. She agrees that he can't just go with being dead.

I think you should leave here, she says, go elsewhere.

That is my plan. We are in fact leaving here. But that does not really solve the problem. I'm going to show up in the international newspapers as a corpse. That won't do. I will have to send out some people and say someone has been impersonating me, he says. I hate making things like this up. It's weak. Sometimes one has to. This is a sloppy world, but if I can avoid such lies, I will.

It's not how I wanted it to end, he continues, and she still can't tell whether he has truly been shaken up, or whether it is just a passing problem that he will throw money at to overcome. If she could see his face, surely she would know.

At the foot of the bridge that night, as she watched the two men grapple and the one get thrown into the river, she sees what Caslon can't see. The victor crosses through traffic to the other side of the bridge and looks over the downriver edge, anticipating his double's materialization. She wonders what she is witnessing, horrified enough by what the men were doing to each other to contemplate breaking her verbal agreement and contacting the police. Not running away though, she waits, and sees what the man on the bridge – her Caslon – cannot see: a figure in the river swimming toward one of the party boats. Moments later Caslon returns, cutting past as though to pull her again into his gravitational field, and she follows, having already decided that she could say nothing about the swimmer since it was something beyond the scope of Caslon's experience. It was implicit to her that she was not to see anything that Caslon did not. That was her way of being faithful to his memoir. But in her attempt to banish the image from her mind she simply reinforces it, turning it into a repetitive loop. Moreover, the second Caslon's watery flight, she realizes, showed an in-dependence that compelled her to applaud him, to silently rally for him, the discarded man.

You know what is strange about us? Caslon says, his mood shifting, lightening. He no longer seems concerned for what he's done, or about his body washing ashore.

We have something in common, he says. It seems unlikely, and someone looking at us from the outside would never recognize it, but we have something valuable for its similarity. It's not just that we are here together in a boat or that we've shared some experiences. It's that we are both able to do this, what we've been doing on land, in a foreign city far from our homes. We are both free and independent enough to have gone about without obligations to anyone else. No one is preventing us from doing this, telling us that they need us, that what we are doing is impossible because of our schedules. We are not tied to some outside thing. That is what makes us similar.

I can see how you might believe that, Etti says.

Look at how we are together. We don't have jobs, really. I've given you a job that's hardly work, and *I* don't have a job other than to oversee my investments and the people that I employ, all in a very cursory way.

And we are of the same vintage. We are like two sides of the same coin.

Yet it is true, he goes on, and likely very important, that I have all the money in the world, and you, until you met me, basically had none. I am somehow outside of something because I have so much money, and you are somehow outside of something because you have none.

I don't feel that we are all that similar, Etti says. I feel like we are on two different plains of existence. That we have strangely intersected, but not because we are similar. I'm open to the idea, though.

You're right, we are fundamentally different. In so many basic categories we are different. You're a woman. And you're brownish, olivish – dark, people would have said in the past. And I'm a kind of white. And that difference, I admit, makes you so valuable to me. You wouldn't be here if not for that difference. Here I am saying we are very similar and then I go on and say we are very different. But.

Caslon continues, shifting his weight enough to rock the boat: In another era I could have written this memoir myself. I would have been the source of all authority about myself and people would have tried to understand my words exactly as I meant them. I would have been long-winded and opinionated, and free with what I had to say. I might even have been offensive to some. And in an era that came later I would have been more self-conscious in my writing, and someone would have said to disregard my authority entirely, to do what you would with my words, interpret them as you would. Readers were so powerful in that era. But in this era, our present time, it's not about what I say. Not really. It's about what I am. I am a rich man. The truth is in my presence, not in what I say. Or what I say is true *because* of my presence.

And so when it comes to us: isn't it that much better that you are both a poor woman and dark, or whatever, whereas I'm white and wealthy. No one cares if I speak, he says. Well, of course lots of people care if I speak. However I'm not thinking of all those people who care when I speak. When I speak it means something different from when you speak. By making you my author, I've made my life so much more important. More present. I've given it so much more dimension.

Things that Etti might have let pass in other situations she can't let pass here. They are central to whatever Caslon is trying to explain. She says, Those are really your emphases, not mine. I'd prefer not to think of myself or you in those terms.

That only adds to it, he says.

I would really like to remove my blindfold, Caslon.

Please don't, he says. It's really much better that you don't. It's just very bright and watery out here. Let me finish what I was saying: Doesn't this prove my point about us and our generation: that we depend on each other for our meaning. That we really are two sides of the same coin. Maybe contradictory sides. That is Zidane. He shows contradictory sides existing in a single person in a single action. And this contradiction spoke to our generation. But sometimes a single person cannot generate such contradictions within himself. Sometimes he needs a second person.

Are you satisfied with your memoir so far? she asks.

Very satisfied. Of course. I'm extremely satisfied with it. But you know what I have realized? Caslon says. That the memoir was best at the beginning.

How do you mean? she asks.

It was most dynamic in the first days. I have no doubt about that. Then something changed. I think I've come up with the answer to why that's the case: that you are most perfect when you don't have money.

Etti waits for him to continue.

I know that you must have changed though I don't know exactly how. The mind changes with money. I do know this: the closer you get to me, financially speaking, the less effective you are at your job.

Of course you are miles and miles away from me, Caslon continues, and you will never get anywhere near me in terms of wealth. And yet, there is this paradox: the more I pay you, the less effective you become. Do you see what I mean? The more money you earn, the smaller the space between us becomes, and the smaller the space between us, the narrower my life appears. You know I want the widest experience possible. If you were working for free, and therefore had basically no money at all, you would be the perfect memoirist, because there would be the greatest space between us for you to observe me in.

Etti feels alone on the opposite side of the boat from him, but she tries to understand his logic. She believes that she follows it, beyond it being a ploy to pay her nothing – in fact there is not really a scheme to pay her nothing, as he could afford to pay a thousand Ettis to author his memoir. She tries to remain open to the idea that underlies the proposal, and from one angle even says yes to it. This is the thing, she likely thinks. This is what I've been looking for without knowing it. And F is there in her mind thinking she is crazy, saying things get so tacky when the super-wealthy are involved and that this is no exception. They always get their way. You need to direct your energy with great care, F says. And Etti agrees with her. But maybe this is also where she and F sharply diverge in their ways of thinking. Isn't this exactly the thing I've been looking for, she says to F. This is what I've been looking for because it is a shocking change from what I've been doing. That is why, F says, you shouldn't do it. It doesn't feel like your work.

I've learned so much from you, Etti, Caslon says, and I wish that you could stay at my side for a long time. But this is an issue that has really only a single solution in my mind. What do you think?

Late that night of the bridge, back at their hotel, Etti observed Caslon flipping through the books on his bedside table and not settling into anything. He turned off the lamp and seemed to fall asleep immediately. The image of the two men grappling continued to play in her head, keeping her up, and she wondered how inevitable the scene really was. She spent the first hour of the night trying to convince herself that it was in no way inevitable.

Isn't it true, she thought, late that hour, that if Caslon had simply been patient, the second Caslon would have become more and more dissimilar to him so that everyone would recognize that the second was not Caslon at all? This drift had already started – Caslon had said as much and Etti had seen it first-hand. Every distinct and separate experience they had would subtly transfigure them, and the ongoing result would be difference, continual differentiation, so that outsiders would come to see two completely different people. That would have been such a gift to both of them, she thought.

And in this realization Etti found herself again siding with the second Caslon, hoping that, when he pulled himself up onto the party boat in the middle of the great river, hands grabbing at his wet clothing to help him out, and when he returned to his hotel room and did whatever he did there, that he would irreversibly excise his being from Caslon's.

Surely this was possible, she thought.

Later that night she took out the Dutch vacation postcard she had intended for Gil. She began writing with *Dear Gil* and didn't know where to go from there. It was important for her to send a message – the very act of sending the message would likely fulfill something that was eating away at her – but she didn't know what to write. I'm all tiredness, she thought, and put the postcard and the pen away under her cot. She would remember to bring it with her when they left the hotel.

Victoria

In that moment of release, at that very breath she screams 'out there,' I pop up against the sliding glass door of the condo balcony, clothed as I had been the morning I left Classplaza. My parts feel no different, I don't hum with revivification, yet the movement now is all mine. My arms go out to her. Before I think of anything else, I offer myself in loving embrace.

Though I hold this gesture and continue to look down at her with tenderness, hoping that we could have a moment, the moment that we have both so well earned having survived this greatest intimacy together, she does not move. We have come so far. She has started speaking to me, and I have managed at long last to speak to her. But she inspects me as though I were a stranger or an intruder, shuddering and cowering below me, and I stay where I am, looking down upon her, waiting for her to acknowledge our connection before I leave. Her silence grows into a mix of disgust and offence. And I push it, I wait too long, because now she can do nothing but speak her mind, shouting at me to go, perhaps in recognition that I am her aborted shadow, a truly horrific sight for her.

I depart without another word.

Etti

Etti holds the slack blindfold in her hand, adjusting to the overly illuminated deck of the *Nancy*, with its broad continuum of pastel planks and network of stainless-steel railings. Caslon forms the centre of her view, luminous in his white shirt, larger than life, seemingly taking pleasure in her squinting vulnerability. He says that they can talk more if she likes. Come find me, he says, when you've made your decision. I'll be here. As he leaves her, Nelson appears by her side.

She has her former quarters again, her collection of things still in the drawer where she left it. She deposits the new blind, the postcard, her clutch and the bank card.

In what unfold as distracted, restless days before Etti speaks to Caslon again, the 1%/99% woman becomes a locus for Etti's uneasiness. In the dining hall and corridors there are no signs of her, there is never any answer at the woman's quarters, the games room is always locked.

One night she wakes with an urgent need to speak to the woman. Something had been performed, she decides. The woman had been a performer of her story. Something was faked.

Despite all the things that must have been made up in the story, she thinks, there was also something very true about it. She recognizes herself in the woman, the simplest of correspondences – they are both women without much money, brought on board the superyacht *Nancy* by these men with so much money. And they weren't brought on board as prostitutes or maids, but for ambiguous purposes. To satisfy something more for the men. Her world was somehow aligned with the other woman's. Maybe the woman also had a project that she was keeping to herself. And now Etti wonders, if there were indeed a project, whether the woman had abandoned it or managed to complete it. More likely abandoned, she thinks.

On deck the night sky is darker than it has been, the summer has progressed and stars appear. Nelson hangs around at the top of the stairs, her constant, if useless, silent companion.

One afternoon she goes through her collection: the blindfolds, her costume, the rubbing, her **ОКАДБ** bank card, the silver clutch, the pen from the bridge, the old copy of the *Financial Times*. She lays her costume flat on her bed and configures the rest of the objects around it. She assembles parts of the rubbing to spell out its phrases. The materials frustrate her. They don't do anything for her.

And with a resolution to abandon her objects, Caslon's proposal creeps into view. In spite of all the signs that she should do otherwise, she begins to sway, has an unnamable compulsion toward him. To return to him not for the job, but for the piece that would come out of it. For the project. It is a project that needs nothing added to it, she likely thinks. It is perfect in its simplicity. In a sense, Caslon perfected it. When she has finished with Caslon, she thinks, it will be a real work. She tries to let her intuition speak, removing herself as best as she can, and this is what it tells her. A real work, though one with zero documentation. She tries to imagine how to represent something that exists only in the time of her rigorous watch. Without documentation it would be as if it never happened.

Is not all of this openness to others, F says, just an accommodation of their desires at the expense of your own? I mean, aren't you just enabling him? And Etti is thrilled at F's argument against her, because it feels truly like someone else saying no to her decision, not just her own second self. Yes, Etti says back to her. I want to see what happens when this person's desires prevail. No! F says, and disappears from her mind.

Objects put away, except for the postcard. She writes the Classplaza address to the right of the postcard's dividing line and leaves the area on the left, below *Dear Gil*, empty. There is really only one thing to write on this, and in an uncharacteristic display of acting without thinking, she folds the card in half before leaving it in the drawer, having finally put a few words on it.

-plaza

Neither of us was looking for an ideal outcome if it involved, at its core, the conjunction of a woman and a man into a singular consciousness outside of all earthly experience, on the moon, or on Mars or Pluto or some other kind of place entirely, virtual or real, whatever the present equivalent might be. Even if the outer-spatial picture were removed, if it simply meant a conflation of life here on earth, we were not looking for it.

That ideal belonged to another generation, one shown to us in a black and white photo: long hair and loose clothes, standing in a field with a metal pod glinting sunlight in the background. Their generation amounted to fifteen or twenty years out of thousands that swept over us. And yet. We have dismissed their ideal only to revive its opposite. Now we surely aim to be opposing parties, cut away from each other, utterly discrete. We aim to come together in opposition. The ideal outcome of humanity, our utopia, I think as I ponder Etti's latest wasteland, lies in the inviolable gap that separates us.

This new place is so utterly terrifying to me, I can't imagine why I came. But I did come to it on my own. I sought her out.

I could never have foreseen a place with no horizon. Even a closed room with no windows has walls that become a proxy horizon, a very near one, and suggest a space on the outside that has a distant but visible line separating our ground from our heavenly potential. But these precisely curved walls . . . It was not obvious to me on my arrival, but as I continue to take it all in, to smell its old cement, after days of habitation, I see this complete absence of a special place to plant our futurity as Etti's master stroke. I don't know how she has come to pull this off, how she has learned to do this. She makes it look effortless.

I leave Etti to do her work in front of the computer. If in the past she was concerned that I was outside of life, that I was not looking for stable work, that I spent all my time with books and stuck in my own head, now she seems not to care in the least. She leaves me to myself, barely acknowledging my arrival. Maybe we have achieved another level of togetherness emptied of that thing that for so long caused us friction. It feels like an entirely new territory for us.

After my departure from Victoria, I sought out the moon man and woman martian. When Victoria and I were out on the street after she'd abandoned their offers, I recognized the neighbourhood, even the industrial-era factory they'd hauled us into was familiar. Years ago I'd been there. It was a preparty, maybe even for the turn of the millennium. I remember sinking into a worn-out couch, people coming in and out of rooms, putting on their party costumes, others arriving and drinking beer, music playing from speakers suspended from the beams in the ceiling. People getting up to change the records, people doing things together in the bathroom, people shouting yeah! with each arrival. It must have gone on like this for hours, our numbers growing and the room becoming loud with conversation. I would have been twenty-five or so and everyone else was around that age. And Etti must have been there with me, at the birth of our relationship, when it was all inexhaustable newness. At the time I must have felt that everything I needed in the world was right there in that room with those people in their tight party-ready outfits, with Etti and her overflowing youthful everything. And I'm sure that I required no thought of a future self. Everything I needed was there.

So much is going on in the picture that I can't articulate. That young Gil is so assimilated in his environment, I can barely see where he ends and everything else begins.

I took the elevator to the third floor and found their door. I knocked and waited. No one answered, and I waited some more, then did something I never do. I tried the door. It opened and I looked into the space that was exactly as I remembered it, with sunlight streaming in through the leaves of plants, the great beams and all the nice furniture. I entered the main area with its chairs and couches. Hello there, I said loudly. Had they been there I don't know what I would have said to them, what I would have said to the woman martian. I stood staring at all the things, wondering why I was not leaving right away, wondering why I desired something in it so hopelessly. And I waited until I could no longer stand myself. It was then that I saw the copy of *One-Dimensional Man* on the coffee table on top of a stack of magazines. The giant black 'i' on the cover was monolithic but also comic for its blunt depiction. I went over to hold it in my hands, to read the back cover. I flipped it open to a page where a few sentences had been underlined in pencil: *The vamp, the national hero, the dark listless wanderer, the dissenting employee . . . They are no longer images of another way of life but rather useful anomalies of the same life, serving as an affirmation rather than negation of the established order. All horizons have been assimilated by what has been here either for a long time, or just for a few hours before we arrived.*

I thought, was this the moon man's or the woman martian's underlining? Or perhaps some long previous owner's?

I returned the book to the stack of magazines and said to myself that when I finally left the apartment, closing the door would be like closing the covers of a '60s paperback. But it is not as easy as that.

The night Etti and I share a bottle of beer, we sit on the cold pitted floor watching videos on YouTube, and I begin massaging the middle of her back. I raise her sweater up and cup her breast with my hand as I might have done in our prehistory, almost to conjure something from far away. At the sweater's edge

I see a tattoo crossing her shoulder blade. I've never seen it before. I push her sweater up higher and then she removes her arm from her sleeve and lets the sweater bunch by her neck. The full image runs visibly over her skin: a ship's black anchor, bannered with text. *When We Lived in 3 and 4 Dimensions*, it reads.

She says it's temporary, but clearly it has been absorbed into her cells, under her skin. She slides her arm back into her sweater.

When she speaks again, her tone changes. She says, I tried something that was very difficult, and I broke the agreement that I had made with someone, and so I failed at that thing. I told the person, after months of following him around, that I was becoming too much like him. And he couldn't see what I meant, but I said that how could I not be? I was with him all the time, without end. I had grown to love him and grown to hate him. And I became him. And those things that still made us inviolably different, what he had seen as my most perfect qualities, had become so tainted . . . When I faltered in my work I think he started hating them, those qualities, as though they were to blame. I said as much to him, and he was offended, and he reminded me that those were my perfect qualities. And I said, Maybe we are entering a new era, and he said, I don't see that, not yet. And, I said, I believe we will never experience that moment you are looking for, the Zidane moment or whatever it is that will marry us to the same generation. I actually believe we are too old for that to happen, I said. He said I was being weak, that I was a quitter. But perhaps he believed me. Perhaps I made him doubt himself. He said he was through with people like me. So I was given a golden handshake and let go. I shed some tears over that, but he had none for me. I had been perfect and then I became flawed.

The whole time, I'd had a secondary plan, a project, and now I know it will never be realized. Or it has already been realized, and no one will know about it. I thought it would be the real thing. I thought I'd impress F with my daring and my persistence. But it truly is as if the project never existed.

I've been thinking about what to call our new home, I say to her, and before I tell her what it is she says we should keep thinking about it, she doesn't want to name it yet.

She turns and faces me. Her eyelids hood halfway down her eyes, creating a straight line across their midpoint. This is the first I have really looked at her face in quite some time. She has aged.

I found this place and decided it was for you, she says. And you came. There's a project that I want to do. With you this time. We will come up with everything together. The name of the project we'll come up with, and the name of the place.

I say yes to her, though I wonder if I'm ready for one of her projects, to be the subject of it. I trust her but the offer makes me fear that I'm forever fated to be part of someone else. But I don't voice my concerns. We have known each other for so long I act as though she can read my mind, as though she understands my misgivings, but she really does not.

Good, she says. And we drink the rest of the beer.

Out of my memory chamber emerges what I decide must be the final remnant of Jan Melbrooks' speech. I don't even know if he says it. I can't picture him saying it, but I hear it in his effusive onstage voice:

There are heroes in the world, in history, and there are victims too. We'll begin with the victim: who is he really? The unlucky person who other people hurt? No, that is not what I mean. The one who takes the blame while others around him profit? No, not that either. The one from a bad home, or thrown into terrible circumstances beyond his control? No. None of those. The victim is the one who is blind to his situation, who is manipulated by others, not because other people are bad, but because he is unable to see the potential of his situation. He cannot read his world around him, his present. The zeitgeist remains invisible to him. He is ignorant. Perhaps he is blissful in his ignorance, filling his days with pleasant food and video games. He goes to work and doesn't try to understand how to better his situation. Through his ignorance he becomes objectified by his situation. He becomes an object of history, unimportant, and most importantly, forgotten even as he lives.

And then there is the hero. He has an uncanny ability to feel the present, to read the world, to sense the zeitgeist. He understands that you can't argue with the zeitgeist, but, all the same, you can affect it. He doesn't sit around playing video games or soaking in hot tubs. He is empowered by the potential of his situation. He is the active agent. He uses his insight into the present to change the present – to form a new present. He is the subject of history and will be remembered.

One always buries the most difficult parts. They need to be put out of mind. But now that this one has emerged it sits with me, like a person lurking behind me, for some time. A serious person, brighter than anything I could imagine.

And then it happened. The world was always watching, almost everything. The enclosure that some of our parents had called Spaceship Earth was watching. Even we saw it happen. No one was expecting it.

It was just a simple photograph.

The world was talking about this photo, focused on it, and people were writing about it, and on the radio and TV asking experts to talk about it. It was clear that the photo meant different things to different people, some people taking it as sacred, others as a political game changer. No one could deny its power.

After the beer, we step out the front door of our latest home and walk for a long time. We come to a crowd that has gathered. They are holding candles in their hands, and it is dark out, and we know without asking what it is all about.

The photograph that everyone had seen was galvanizing young people. It spoke to youth. They could see themselves in it, it captured their lack of hope.

While I try to understand what exactly in that picture has compelled them to come, Etti approaches the crowd. She speaks to one of the people, a young man, and they hug each other. From my distance I can only imagine it is one of her teens. I see, among those gathered, a reproduction of the photo that has brought everyone out. I don't know why it has affected them all so deeply. And I don't know whether to feel happy for them in their togetherness, or to doubt what they are doing. I don't know whether to turn away from them, to let this energized gathering fall into the past, or whether to become absorbed by it.

Acknowledgments

Thank you to my early readers: Jacob Wren, Tamara Faith Berger, Simon Rogers, Alex Licker, Amber Yared. Thank you to Jay MillAr and Hazel Millar for all the exceptional things they do and to Ruth Zuchter for her super eye.

Thank you to the OAC Writers' Reserve for financially supporting the writing of this novel.

An excerpt of the novel was published in a different form by *Eleven Eleven* journal. Thank you to the editors.

The lines from Herbert Marcuse's *One-Dimensional Man*, appearing on page 200, have been altered from the original.

Colophon

Distributed in Canada by the Literary Press Group:
www.lpg.ca

Distributed in the United States by Small Press Distribution:
www.spdbooks.org

Shop online at www.bookthug.ca

Designed by Malcolm Sutton
Typeset in Parkinson Electra and Nitti Grotesk
Copy edited by Ruth Zuchter

BOOK
PRODUCTION
WAR ECONOMY
STANDARD